THE POSSIBILITIES OF SAINTHOOD

The POSSIBILITIES OF SAINTHOOD

DONNA FREITAS

FRANCES FOSTER BOOKS

FARRAR, STRAUS AND GIROUX

NEW YORK

www.fsgkidsbooks.com

Library of Congress Cataloging-in-Publication Data

Freitas, Donna.

The possibilities of sainthood / Donna Freitas.—1st ed.

p. cm.

Summary: While regularly petitioning the Vatican to make her the first living saint, fifteen-year-old Antonia Labella prays to assorted patron saints for everything from help with preparing the family's fig trees for a Rhode Island winter to getting her first kiss from the right boy.

ISBN-13: 978-0-374-36087-0

ISBN-10: 0-374-36087-1

[1. Saints—Fiction.   2. Italian Americans—Fiction.   3. Family life—Rhode Island—Fiction.   4. Catholic schools—Fiction.   5. Schools—Fiction.   6. Conduct of life—Fiction.   7. Rhode Island—Fiction.]   I. Title.

PZ7.F8844 Pos 2008

[Fic]—dc22

2007033298

In memory of three special made-up saints in my life who've gone on to that great palace in the sky:

my academic mentor, Monsignor Stephen Happel,
the Patron Saint of High Places

my grandmother, Amalia Goglia,
the Patron Saint of Artichokes and People Who Say Yes When
Mom and Dad Say No

and most especially
my mother, Concetta Lucia Freitas,
the Real Patron Saint of People Who Make Pasta

PART 1

The Patron Saint of Figs and Fig Trees

Vatican Committee on Sainthood
Vatican City
Rome, Italy

November 1

To Whom It May Concern (ideally the Pope if he's available):

I'm writing to inform you of a serious oversight in the area of patron saint specializations. As yet, there is no Patron Saint of Figs and Fig Trees. I mean, I know over there in Italy they practically grow wild and all because of the idyllic climate, but let me tell you, trying to keep fig trees alive through a Rhode Island winter requires divine intervention. Do you have any idea what we have to do when it starts to get cold? Not only do we have to prune them, we have to bury them! Let me be clear: come winter, I, that's me, Antonia, BURY our fig trees. Have you ever tried to bury a tree? It's not exactly an afternoon job. Of course, it's worth it when those yummy, succulent figs start bursting to life come springtime. (Yes, that's right: spring. It's miraculous really. Our figs, the LABELLA family figs, show up in springtime, not summer!) But anyway, I think it would really help Catholic fig growers all over the world and especially in Rhode Island if we had a Patron Saint of Figs, because, Lord knows, I'd pray to this saint. I mean, if we can have a Patron Saint AGAINST CATERPILLARS (Caterpillars? What's so bad about caterpillars?), I don't think a saint specializing in figs is too much to ask.

Thank you for your attention to this matter.

Blessings,
Antonia Lucia Labella
Labella's Market of Federal Hill
33 Atwells Avenue
Providence, RI USA
saint2b@live.com

P.S. Incidentally, if you are looking for someone to fill these particular shoes, that would be those of the new Patron Saint of Figs, I'd be delighted to take the job. In fact, I insist! I can be reached by e-mail, or you could always just come by the market. Anyway, what I am trying to say is that if you need to get in touch with me, I'm easy to reach. Hope to hear from you soon!

1

I Pray to St. Sebastian About Gym Class and Thank God I'm Not Named After the Patron Saint of Snakebites

I gazed up at the familiar boy. A golden aura surrounds his beautiful, muscular body, arrows poking into him from every direction.

Poor saint, I thought to myself. I hope it doesn't hurt.

Sebastian's stare was piercing, as if he were looking right through me. As if his gaze were another arrow pointed my way.

I closed my eyes but the image stayed. It should. The picture of St. Sebastian had been hanging on the wall in our living room for as long as I could remember, right near the old-fashioned record player my mother listened to when she was dusting all the other saint statues and figurines, her daily tribute to the men and women who watch over us. Occasionally I'd come home from school and Mom would be belting out "That's Amore" or "Volare" in her just-off-the-boat Italian accent. I had to be careful not to bring anyone up to the apartment when I heard music

playing, or they might think she was crazy. She's a charac-
ter, my mother.

But then, all Catholics are a weird bunch. Especially
the Italian ones.

I opened my eyes and read quietly from my Saint Diary.

Dear St. Sebastian:

O Patron Saint of Athletes, please
help me not look stupid tomorrow in
gym class when we play soccer even
though I am not very fast, kick the
ball in the wrong direction occasionally, and sometimes forget which team
I'm on. And I promise I won't sit down
out on the field this time if they make
me play defense again and I get bored.
Ideally, I'd like to play more like Hilary, our star soccer player (even
though she is named after the Patron
Saint of Snakebites). But if I can't be
as good as Hilary, I'll settle for just not
getting picked last. And don't forget
about Mrs. Bevalaqua. It would be really great if her arthritis got better so
she could walk again. Thank you, St.
Sebastian, for your intercession in
these matters.

I lit the worn-down pillar candle beneath sexy Sebastian and gave him a longing look, as if I could will him to step out of his frame. It was right about then that my moment alone with the half-naked, holy babe was interrupted.

"Time to get ready for bed, Antonia! It's getting late and you have school tomorrow," Mom yelled from the kitchen.

"I'm *praying*," I called back, my voice all "Please don't interrupt my saint time," aware that the surest way into whatever flexibility my mother could offer was through piety.

"Five more minutes, then!"

I started to close my diary when I noticed that the corner of my St. Anthony mass card was peeling. I smoothed the edge gently, lovingly, as if I were brushing the cheek of Andy Rotellini, the boy I'd been in love with since the summer before ninth grade. A crease was beginning to mark the murky blue sky surrounding Anthony, dark against the gleam of his halo. I dipped my pinkie into the pool of hot wax around the candlewick and placed a tiny drop on the corner of the card, refastening it to the page. Below St. Anthony's image was a pocket made of thick, red linen paper, stuffed with devotions and prayers, some on random scraps of this and that, others scribbled on colorful Post-its. Anthony's page had more devotions than any other saint in my diary.

My Saint Diaries were my most sacred possessions.

"*I'm praying*, Mommy," said a voice behind me, sing-song and catty, sending a shiver up my spine. Not the scary sort of shiver or even the good kind, but the "blech" kind you felt when you met up with something disgusting. "I'm such a good little holier-than-thou girl, *Mommy*," the voice went on, its nasal tone like nails against a chalkboard.

"Veronica," I said, whirling around to face my cousin — who also starred as the evil nemesis in my life, not to be overly melodramatic or anything, because it is totally true. Veronica is eVil with a capital V. I tucked my Saint Diary behind me, making sure it was hidden.

Veronica was at the apartment trying to learn some of the Italian cookie recipes from my mother because *her* mother, my aunt Silvia, was determined that at least one of her three daughters would turn out to be a kitchen natural and grow up to usurp *my* mother at the family store. I'd thought I could successfully avoid Veronica's visit, but I was wrong. My blood began to boil, but I took comfort in the fact that Veronica's outfit was way too tight and her hair was so teased and sprayed that she was the caricature of a Rhode Island Mall Rat. "Remember when you used to be a nice person and people like me could actually stand to be around you?" I asked, once I knew my temper was in check.

"Remember when *you* used to *not* be such a total baby?" Sarcasm oozed from Veronica's voice. Something — maybe almond paste? — was smeared down the side of her face. I bet she squeezed it straight from the tube into her mouth like a greedy glutton. "You and your mother think you're so high and mighty."

"Veronica . . ." my mother was calling. "Veronica? If

you are not here to watch, you are never going to learn how to fold these egg whites into the batter properly . . . Yoohoo! Where are you?"

"Yeah, yeah, I'm coming, Auntie," she said, rolling her eyes and disappearing back down the hall. Her footsteps thudded against the wood floor. Thud. Thud.

My cousin, the elephant.

As soon as Veronica was gone, the tension disappeared from my body. I grabbed my Saint Diary from where I'd stashed it and sighed with relief.

My Saint Diaries were also my most *secret* possessions.

Each year on my birthday, February 14, St. Valentine's Day, I began a new volume, fixing different colored pockets onto the pages of a thick book, compiling a section marked "Notes" for my new saint ideas (like a Patron Saint of Homework or a Patron Saint of Notice—as in "Notice me, please, Andy Rotellini!"). Most important of all, I chose which out of the many thousands of official saints to venerate during the year. Tradition, *my* tradition, dictated that St. Anthony of Padua, the Patron Saint for Lost Things, got page number one. Always.

Volume 8, the record of my fifteenth year, was rose red, my favorite color.

In the back was a section for the occasional, precious response letter from the Vatican. (Really they were rejection letters, but I liked to think of them as responses because that sounded less depressing.) I held on to these to remind myself that at least they knew I existed. For the hope that one day, I might just get through to them.

9

You know, *The Vatican People.*

Any day now, the news would arrive. My Patron Saint of Figs proposal was a winner. I could feel it.

"Antonia! *Sbrigati!*" my mother yelled, shattering this moment of hope with her I'm-getting-angry voice and an Italian command that loosely translated as "Get your butt off to bed immediately and don't tell me you're still praying because I won't buy it this time." Early bedtime somehow applied to me but not my cousin.

I faced Sebastian one last time, the heat of the candle flame warm on my chin. "St. Sebastian," I whispered, gazing into his blue eyes, "if you can help me figure out the saint thing, I'd really appreciate it. It's already been thirteen days since I sent the last letter."

"Antonia Lucia Labella!" (That's "lou-chia," by the way, like the pet.)

"Okay, one *more* last thing," I said, tempting the full force of Mom's rage, my lips level with Sebastian's now, as if we were about to kiss. "Even though I *know* that *technically* in the Catholic church you have to be dead to be a saint, I really don't want to die if you can help it. Fifteen is too young to die."

I blew out the candle. A thin stream of smoke drifted up from the blackened wick, reaching toward heaven, and I wondered if I'd soon follow, joining all those who'd gone before me.

In a manner befitting a saint.

2

My Mother Calls Me a Prostitute, Which Is Code for "Antonia, You Look Sexy Today," and I Ask St. Denis the Beheaded Bishop for Assistance

Antonia! You are *not* going out like that!"

"What are you talking about, Mom?" I answered, trying to sound innocent and all. Who me? Have I done something wrong? I was tiptoeing through the front hall hoping to get out the door unnoticed on my way to school.

"Antonia! Don't you dare take another step!"

I looked behind me. Mom was leaning against the doorway between the foyer and the kitchen, staring at my legs, upset as usual about the state of my school uniform. I shoved my hand into my backpack to locate the socks she was going to make me wear despite any protests.

"O *Madonna*! Your bare legs! I can see so much thigh you may as well not be wearing a skirt!" She was using her it's-the-end-of-the-world voice, her left hand moving spastically as she talked. Her dark, roller-filled hair jiggled like a pile of fresh-made gnocchi on its way to the table, as her head shook with disapproval. "My daughter looks like a *puttana*! What have I done to deserve this?"

Important Italian Vocab to Note:

Madonna refers to *the* Madonna, aka, the *real* virgin, not the "Like a Virgin" Madonna, the famous pop star. It's pronounced "ma-dawn," heavy on the *n*, drop the last *a*.

Puttana is Italian for "prostitute" and is known to fly out of my mother's mouth in my direction. I like to think of it as a compliment. You know, my mother's special way of noting out loud that her daughter is looking particularly sexy at the moment.

"Calm down, Ma," I said, resisting the urge to roll my eyes. Every day on my way to school I'd try to sneak out the door in what my best friend Maria and I regarded as coolness of the uniform, that is, as cool as we could possibly make our yellow, green, and white pleated plaid skirt and matching Catholic schoolgirl gear. And every day Mom would tell me I looked like a streetwalker (her favorite English synonym for *puttana*).

Then we'd argue.

"Are you showing off for the boys, Antonia?" I glanced over my shoulder to find my grandmother in the living room watching me, giggling, swaying in her rocking chair, her tiny body wrapped tight in her old blue bathrobe. Her white frizzed-out hair was styled like she might be auditioning for the part of Einstein's mother.

I felt my face turn red.

"Gram! Sshhh," I pleaded, giving her a meaningful look. "You're not helping." Gram had lived with Mom and me in the apartment above the family store since Dad died when I was seven. She was partly to blame for my saint obsessions. Her bedroom was filled with icons, mass cards, and pillar-candle shrines. A glass-domed porcelain baby Jesus dressed as a king with a big fancy crown and flowing red robes—the Infant of Prague—sat center stage on her bureau. Gram's room was like a shrine.

"And after you find those socks you are going to unroll that skirt until I can't see even an inch of thigh!" Mom stepped toward me as if she was going to do the uniform adjustment herself.

"Ma! Seriously. I'll fix everything when I get to school," I said, but my pleas were futile. She was staring at my waist with the look of a bull about to charge. "Nobody else goes to school in uniform. You should see Veronica and Concetta . . ." Concetta was Veronica's sister, the middle child of my wicked trio of cousins. Francesca was the third and the oldest.

"I don't care about your cousins and that is your aunt Silvia's business if she wants to let her daughters leave the house half-naked."

My mother had gone to a Catholic girls' school, too— starting in sixth grade, when her family immigrated from Napoli—and in every picture she's in textbook uniform: sensible brown shoes, kneesocks stretched until the threads are about to snap, plaid skirt lengthened to below the knee, so that bare skin is totally hidden, long-sleeved oxford shirt buttoned up to her chin. My mother always looked perfect and *virginal*. I might be *technically* virginal, but that didn't mean I needed to look that way.

All Normal Catholic Schoolgirls had creative ways of sluttifying our pure-as-the-driven-snow required attire.

Catholic Girl's Guide to Uniform Alteration

1. Most important is rolling your skirt so that it is a virtual mini (you keep folding it over at the waistband).

The key to successful skirt rolling is to be sure your Catholic pleated plaid is already hemmed at least two inches above the knee. Otherwise, if you have to fold it over, like, twenty times at the waist, you end up looking as if you've got a serious amount of extra inches around the middle. Not attractive. If you have a mother like mine who insists on skirts at least to the knee, then you have several possible options: get out the ironing board and iron the desired hem, then either tape said hem or carefully safety-pin it all around the bottom, ideally so that none of the pins show through to the front. Why not just pull out a needle and thread and hem it for real? Because you always need to be prepared for emergency hem-letting-down when your mother wonders why your skirt seems so short. If she realizes you illegally hemmed it, getting grounded is almost inevitable.

2. The question of boxer shorts: to wear or not to wear boxer shorts underneath your skirt?

Catholic mothers across the nation hate this trend of girls wearing boxers even more so than the rolling up of the plaid. Preferably, you should buy your own boxers. It's weird to steal from Dad, though some girls do it. I don't know when or who started the boxers craze, but it's been going on for as long as I've been at Catholic school (which is always). To be honest, I don't know why wearing boxers is cool, because sometimes, frankly, it looks kind of bad, but we do it anyway. Still, depending on how much you want the boys to see, boxers are a good preventive measure for the accidental flashing factor.

3. Legs: as bare as possible. Wear socks only when you are made to, and when wearing them, make sure they are scrunched down to the ankles. Never, I repeat, *never* wear tights.

4. Standard white oxford: ideally two buttons undone and never buttoned all the way to the neck. Cute, tight-fitting tank top underneath for before and after school when you are hanging out in the parking lot.

The tank top allows you to remove the required oxford entirely if you so choose and transform yourself into the ideal sexy Catholic schoolgirl that every Catholic schoolboy wants to go out with. Note: Never ever let your mother or teacher/principal see you in just a tank top or you'll be in trouble for sure.

"In my day, the nuns used to measure our skirts!" My mother waved her right hand as she launched into her familiar uniform lecture. I dropped my backpack onto the dark tile of our foyer. It made a satisfying thump when it hit the floor and I struck my best here-we-go-again pose, which involved some hip-jutting, impatient sighing, and foot-tapping. "We had to kneel down on the floor, and if the hem didn't touch the ground we were sent home."

Oh, the drama.

"Yeah, Ma. I know. You've told me. Like eighty times."

"You don't learn to dress like a respectful Labella girl soon and *I'm* going to make you kneel down *every morning* before leaving the house to measure *your* skirt! You just wait." Her hand buzzed around her like a fly. "If your father were still alive . . ."

"Don't even go there, Ma" I said, interrupting, feeling hurt that she would pull the Dad card. "If Dad were around he'd spend more time telling me to have a good day and less time freaking out over stupid things like whether or not I am wearing socks and the exact length of my uniform skirt."

"No respect," she muttered. "You used to be such a nice little girl. What did I do wrong? O *Madonna*!"

I sat down with a huff in an old wooden chair to put on my green socks. Anything to get Mom off my back and myself out the door. I said a quick prayer to St. Denis, the

Patron Saint Against Strife and Headaches, for added assistance (who, incidentally, is usually portrayed holding his head in his hands because he was, well, *beheaded*, and therefore the perfect poster boy for people worrying about headaches).

"St. Agnes, help this child," my mother rambled on, under her breath. St. Agnes is the Patron Saint of Bodily Purity and Chastity, and one of her favorites.

"Pull. Them. Up. Antonia." Mom didn't like the fact that I'd squished my kneesocks down to my ankles. She was in front of me now with hands on hips, her "Kiss the Cook" apron tied around her middle. Dad gave it to her for Christmas one year. She always wore it. There was a smear of flour on her face, which meant she'd been making pasta. She got up at ungodly hours to make it from scratch.

Time to raise the white flag, I decided, stretching my socks to my knees. I stood up and marched toward the door, hoping to get out without any further assaults on my attire.

I had to give Mom credit on at least one count: despite the psychotic behavior, no one else could make pasta like she did. A few pinches of this, a little bit of that, some flour, eggs, and poof! It was like magic. The whole state of Rhode Island pretty much agreed with me, or at least our neighborhood did—Federal Hill, where my family opened Labella's Market more than three decades ago. Between the tourists looking for "authentic Italian" and the neighborhood regulars, we almost couldn't keep my mother's pasta in stock. She inherited that amazing Italian cooking intuition: knowing when whatever you're cooking has "just enough" of this and "just enough" of that. The key to good pasta is "just knowing" the right feel of the dough. There are people in this world who've only had pasta from a cardboard box, who have never felt the warm, soft, floury ball of dough before it is rolled out to be cut. I am sad for these people. When it is made just right, pasta dough is as soft as a down pillow. And despite Mom's constant chastising, I admit that seeing a smear of flour across her forehead gave me a thrill. There was nothing, *nothing* like Mom's fresh homemade pasta.

"Antonia! You'll be at the store at four p.m. sharp, eh?"

"How could I forget, Ma? I have to be there *every* day, same time."

"I don't want Francesca working by herself. She always confuses the pepper biscuits with the *tarallucci*, stupid girl."

"Mom, Francesca can't help the fact that she's a total airhead." I couldn't help agreeing with her about that particular branch of our family tree. I opened the door and felt the cool air that signaled freedom.

"Be there at four," my mother said, unable to resist another reminder.

"I'm leaving, Mother."

"Four!"

I was almost outside when I heard an angry "Antonia!" I froze, afraid to turn around. "Yes, Mother?"

"*What* do we do before leaving the house?"

I took a step back.

"Sorry, Mom, I forgot." I sighed, dipping my finger in the bowl of holy water Mom kept by the doorway and crossing myself.

"You may forget Jesus, Antonia, but *he never forgets you!*"

"Okay, *Ma.*"

She was out of control.

"Bye, *Ma,*" I yelled, exasperated, marching down the stairs and out the side door of Labella's Market without looking back at the giant sign that advertised where we lived. And cooked. And grew figs.

3

I Run into Michael, the Pseudo-Archangel, Who Is So Not Angelic

You're probably thinking that I don't get along with my mother, but that's not exactly true. It isn't that Mom and I have a bad relationship. We really love each other and I know she'd walk to the ends of the earth for me if she had to and all that and vice versa as far as I'm concerned. It's just that ours is a typical Italian mother-daughter relationship.

The Top Five Ways Italians Express Love

1. By always being totally honest with one another, i.e., fighting.

2. Occasionally we scream at each other, which, for Italians, especially between family members, is how you express the fierceness of your love for the other person.

3. Imparting guilt is another popular sign of affection: making someone feel bad about skipping Sun-

day Mass or admonishing your daughter for not making wise decisions about her outfits and potentially embarrassing the entire family, which, of course, she would never want to do.

4. Intense bodily animation, most commonly articulated through incessant talking *at* the person you love without giving them a chance to get a word in edgewise while at the same time gesticulating wildly with your hands.

5. Eating each other's food. And lots of it. Ideally until you can't get up from your chair. Nothing says love to an Italian more than an overfull stomach.

I thought about this, wondering if these lessons in love had scarred me somehow, as I hurried down Atwells Avenue. My books bounced against my back, a reminder that I still had to finish my algebra homework before first period. A gold Mustang raced by, laughter spilling out its open windows. Concetta was driving and Veronica sat on the passenger side. It never occurred to them to offer their poor, only-child cousin a ride to school. I waited at the corner of Atwells and Murphy for a walk signal.

"Antonia! Hello! Over here!" a familiar voice called out.

"Hi, Mrs. B," I said, turning to wave. I couldn't pass our neighbor Mrs. Bevalaqua without a quick hello. Mrs. B had been in a wheelchair because of arthritis for as long as I could remember. She was out catching the last rays of fall sun on her front porch. In full makeup, I might add.

"How are you, *carina*?" *Carina* is Italian for "dear one."

"I'm fine," I said, a little out of breath from leaping up the old wooden staircase. Mrs. B took my hand, squeezing hard. Hers felt bony and brittle. It was spotted with age and blue-gray veins webbed through her skin. Mrs. Bevalaqua's first name was Cecilia, which also was the name of the Patron Saint of Singers and Music, a fitting title for a former opera soprano. Though Mrs. B hadn't been able to sing for years now.

"Do you want a cough drop? I've got your favorite flavor," I said, pulling a lemon one from my bag with my free hand.

"You're such a nice girl, thank you," she said, smiling, her pink lipstick cracking across her lips. She took the cough drop and slipped it into the pocket of her thick brown cardigan.

"Tell that to my mother next time you see her, Mrs. Bevalaqua."

"Don't worry, I will, *carina*. Go on now. I know you need to get to school, but you are sweet to always stop by." She gave my hand a final squeeze before letting go.

"I'll see you later," I said, heading down the stairs two at a time, when suddenly I stopped. Why, I wasn't sure. I ran back up to Mrs. Bevalaqua, sitting there in her wheelchair, dressed to the nines as if she were waiting for a date to take her dancing, and my heart filled with what—sorrow, sympathy, helplessness? I bent down and gave her a soft, quick kiss on the cheek. "It's going to be okay," I whispered, and was down the stairs again in a flash, bag strung across my shoulders.

"Your mother already has my list," Mrs. Bevalaqua called out, referring to the grocery request she'd phoned in at the beginning of the week that I would deliver tonight. "You think there is a fig or two left or are they all gone?"

"I'll see what I can do, okay? We might have something hidden in the kitchen. Have a nice day, Mrs. B," I said, walking backward, waving goodbye until the trees blocked her from view.

A cool breeze picked up, blowing my hair so that I had to keep beating it back from my eyes and mouth, hoping it wouldn't be a tangled mess by the time I got to school. I prayed to Mary Magdalen, the Patron Saint of Hairstylists, for help, but it wasn't doing any good. (Yes, *that* Mary Magdalen.) The fall chill reminded me of the daunting task I had ahead of me this weekend: burying the famous Labella fig trees in the backyard. It would take all day Saturday to prune the thin lattice of branches that hung low around the trunks and almost all day Sunday (not to mention the help of half the neighborhood) to bend what was left of the trees' sturdier but still pliable limbs until they reached the ground. Imagine a person touching their toes with their fingertips, but replace the person with two beautiful old trees reaching their oldest, thickest branches all the way to the soil beneath, a position they would have to endure for an entire season filled with ice and snow. That's basically what it meant to winterize the fig trees, with the final touch of burying them underneath a mountain of canvas and cardboard to protect them from the winter weather until, come springtime, they would yawn and stretch and burst with figs once again.

Sounds poetic, I suppose, but it was a lot of work. Which was also why a Patron Saint of Figs was a great idea.

"Antonia, Antonia!" Little Billy Bruno barreled out the front door of his family's town house. "See," he said, pointing to his elbow, where the outline of a Band-Aid was still visible. The skin inside the rectangle was as good as new. "It's better already!"

"Well, look at that!" I said, laughing. "I told you I could kiss it and make it better."

"You did. It doesn't hurt at all now!"

"Billy, Antonia needs to get to school." Mrs. Bruno appeared on her front porch.

"Hi, Mrs. Bruno," I called out, watching as Billy disappeared back into the house as quickly as he'd come out.

"Thank you for taking care of Billy when he fell yesterday," she said. "He was practically healed by dinnertime. It was so strange . . ."

"Well, you know how kids are . . . crying one minute and fine the next," I said out loud, but inside I was thanking good old St. Amalburga, the Patron Saint Against Arm Pain and Bruising, for her help with Billy. "See you later."

Bright leaves—yellow and red and orange ones—fell like confetti from the trees lining the sidewalks as I passed through the heart of Federal Hill, near Our Lady of

Loreto, the church where my mother met my father back when she was still a Goglia, not a Labella. She was just fifteen at the time and a member of the youth group Dad ran two evenings a week. It was all very scandalous—that my dad was fraternizing with a girl he was supposed to be leading *away* from sin, not toward it. I loved to remind Mom that I was now the same age she was when they started dating. This did not change her opinion about when *I* could start dating, however.

I hurried by Jimmy's Bike Shop, Russo's Grocery (our competition and therefore a place that no one in my family was allowed to patronize), and Antonio's Restaurant, supposedly the best Italian restaurant in all of Federal Hill (they served our homemade pasta, of course). Two old men from the neighborhood were sitting outside at a metal table playing a game of chess, sipping tiny cups of espresso.

"Antonia, *bella*," Mr. Montasero said as I passed. He was about to pick up his queen. "How's Amalia Lucia?"

"She's good. Making pasta as usual," I answered without slowing down.

People were always asking about my mother, Amalia Lucia, always using both of her names. (All three of us—Mom, Gram, and I—had the same middle name, Lucia, which means "light" in Italian and which made the feast day of St. Lucia, the Patron Saint of Light, particularly special in our family.) Ma was kind of a small-town celebrity because of her cooking. *Everybody* knew her. And *everybody* thought she was the greatest. Of course, I had a more nuanced opinion about the woman who disagreed with my dress code, barely let me out after dark, kept me slaving away on a daily basis at the market or otherwise saddled me with *something* store-related, usually along the lines of food preparation. "Antonia! I need help making the eggplant! Where are you going?" she would yell. Or, "Antonia, will you help me roll out this pasta dough for the lasagna?" Or, "Antonia, tonight I am going to teach you how to make the braciola (pronounced like "bra" + "shawl" with a tinge of a *z* sound when you say the "sh" part and you always drop the final *a*) because if I die tomorrow this recipe dies with me and then what would you cook for your children? Tell me! What? What!"

My hand bumped along the fence bordering the park where my best friend, Maria, had kissed John Cronin a few weeks ago after a dance. It must have been romantic — the streetlamps giving off a soft glow, the two of them flirting, pushing each other on the swings, both knowing the evening was certain to end with a kiss. At least that's how Maria told the story. *I* was at home with Mom and Grandma making meatballs for a sauce at the time, a slightly less romantic evening. The only kiss awaiting me was a good-night peck on the cheek from Gram when I wandered off to bed, smelling of meat and olive oil and simmering tomatoes.

You'd think I'd be chubby from all the food, but unlike the other women in my family I'm pretty skinny. I didn't inherit the massive Labella family bosoms like Mom and Grandma either. Even my three cousins got them, while I am particularly lacking in the boob area. The only substantial thing about me is the thick black curls that hang all the way to the middle of my back. Keeping my hair under control was almost as difficult as keeping fig trees alive through the winter, which, by the way, is exactly why the world needs a Patron Saint of Figs and Fig Trees, ASAP.

Somebody, some sympathetic, fig-loving cardinal, was going to read my letter and think, *Hmmm. Figs. This girl Antonia is absolutely right! We need a saint for figs! In fact, Antonia seems like the girl for the job.* Perfetto! Then he would tell the Pope.

I was even named after my favorite saint, Anthony of Padua. Anytime someone lost anything in our house—homework, jewelry, the sugar bowl (that would be due to Grandma)—Mom demanded, "We all need to say a prayer to St. Anthony! St. Anthony will help us find it!" When I was younger I imagined St. Anthony was like a superhero with a cape and leotard and X-ray vision to help him do his miraculous "finding" deeds. But now I just picture him as a young, good-looking spiritual prince watching over me.

Though, truth be told, Mom didn't really do her saint homework and made a teeny-tiny unfortunate mistake when she named me Antonia after St. Anthony. There actually *is* a St. Antonia and she is definitely *not* a finder of lost things. In fact, she died tragically as a teenager. At sixteen. A *virgin*. She actually died *protecting* her virginity, and so it's *very* possible, even highly likely, that she is the Patron Saint of Teenage Purity. So, technically, my name saint is famous for her purity. Her untouched-by-boys-ness.

I am also famous for this, by coincidence.

And though I may accidentally be the pseudo Patron Saint of Teenage Purity, I've been aiming to change Antonia's reputation a bit. Give some color to what is currently an unfortunate and not so exciting association for girls who bear my name. Do a little presainthood damage in the debauchery department and maybe work on my getting a bit less pure in the near future.

"Hey, Antonia," said a voice out of nowhere, startling me.

Michael McGinnis pulled up next to me, driving as slowly as I was walking, hanging out the driver's window of his old, beat-up, hand-me-down Subaru.

"Hi, Michael," I said, but kept walking. That's Michael as in the archangel, picture of innocence and goodness, and McGinnis as in, he's way Irish.

The angel in question and I were friends. Sort of.

"Can I give you a ride, love?" Out of the corner of my eye I saw a smile widen across Michael's freckled face. I could swear he played up the Irish brogue around me on purpose. He called everyone "love," so it's not like his calling *me* "love" made me any different from all the other girls he called "love" on a regular basis—and believe me, there were lots of them.

"No, thanks. I'm almost to school anyway," I said, trying to sound all "normal" and "whatever," willing that he didn't notice the goose bumps that had appeared all over my body the second I heard his voice.

"Come on, Antonia. It would give us a chance to catch up."

"I've got to finish my algebra homework before the first bell," I said, which wasn't exactly a lie, and quickened my pace. I had a rule about Michael: avoid Michael-Antonia-alone-time when possible. Michael and I had *history*.

"I could help," he said in what I was sure he believed was a voice that would tantalize me into accepting. "I'm well past algebra and on to trig, you know . . ."

"I'm not sure I need *your* kind of help, and besides, I'm a math wiz, remember?" I loved math and could practically do it in my sleep. I had Dad to thank for that, who, if he were a saint—even though he never went to college or anything—would definitely have Mathematical Genius on his list of specializations.

"You can't ignore me forever, Antonia, and you know you don't really want to."

"Maybe another time, Michael," I said, turning onto the walking path up to school, signaling the end of our conversation.

"I promise I don't bite, Antonia," he called out hopefully, as if he could change my mind and suddenly I'd decide to get in his car.

"That's not what I've heard," I yelled back.

"How am I going to change your attitude about me?"

"Now, that's something to ponder, Michael."

A car behind him was honking.

"Later, Antonia," he yelled, finally pulling away from the curb.

When I was sure Michael was no longer watching, I turned to see his car heading toward the long, narrow drive leading up to our two high schools. One was all girls (where I went) and looked like your typical 1970s flat-roofed, institutional-style architecture; the other was all boys (where Michael went) and had been around for more than a hundred years, a beautiful Gothic stone mansion with the best sledding hill in all of Rhode Island for a back-yard. Both were Catholic and joined by a shared parking lot, which, by sheer location, was the center of everyone's social universe. Maybe I was more like my name saint than I wanted to admit since I could barely look Michael in the eye. I had good reasons for this, though. Michael tried to kiss me two summers ago but I didn't let him. So now he made me totally nervous. It's also possible that Michael held the honor of being the *only* boy who had ever tried to kiss me. How pathetic is that, to be fifteen and never kissed a boy? Never touched my lips to anyone else's. Never felt their softness melt into mine, which I've been told by Maria is what a good kiss feels like. Never had the chance to bump noses with my beloved, tilting our faces ever so slightly to finally, longingly, taste each other's mouths in a delicious kiss.

Never.

Maybe, by not kissing Michael, I'd missed my only chance. I should've taken advantage of the opportunity while I had it. Even just for practice. Maybe I was doomed to become one of those sweet-sixteen-and-never-been-kissed girls, like poor St. Antonia, the sixteen-year-old dead virgin. It certainly seemed like a miracle was required to get yourself kissed, that's for sure, especially by the boy

I *did* have my eye on, Andy Rotellini, who had never offered me a ride or even made an effort to say more than "hey" in passing.

But I believed in miracles.

You had to if you wanted to become a saint.

4

SISTER NOELLA (POSSIBLY A SECRET
EMISSARY FROM THE VATICAN) TEACHES BIOLOGY
WHILE MARIA AND I PASS NOTES

maria was giving me her ugly face from across the aisle during third-period biology, but it wasn't working since her ugly face wasn't really ugly at all. It's difficult for someone with perfect genes to look unattractive. It was hard not to laugh at her effort, though. She tossed a tiny, crinkled-up piece of paper onto my desk, which I quickly swept into my lap when Sister Noella turned around to write on the whiteboard.

We were learning about dominant and recessive genes, which apparently explained why people like me have brown eyes and people like Maria get blessed with aquamarine ones, but I couldn't help wondering why we didn't spend more time praying to St. Barnabas for world peace or to one of the million saints who intercede on behalf of the sick instead, like St. Maria Mazzarello (not to be confused with *mozzarella cheese*, which has nothing to do with sickness and everything to do with a perfect-tasting lasagna). It would be more useful than figuring out which letters go together in which boxes of the table Sister Noella was enthusiastically drawing so we could tell her if a fruit fly was more likely to have red or white eyes and misshapen or normal wings.

I was busy watching Sister Noella's post–Vatican II short blue habit bounce behind her and contemplating how exactly a nun became a biologist when it occurred to me that maybe Sister Noella wasn't really a biology teacher at all. *Maybe* she was a special envoy sent by The Vatican People to assess my saintly potential. *Maybe* that would explain why Sister Noella was always coming into the store to buy my grandma's weird homemade garlic health remedies instead of going to a drugstore for normal medicine like everybody else. You'd think a biologist would have better sense than to trust a woman like Gram, who regularly clipped stories from tabloids about miraculous two-headed babies and the wonderful healing powers of the sardine. But, then again, maybe Sister Noella was just being nice to Gram. At least, that's what I was thinking when Maria began whispering, "Hey, hey, Antonia . . . Antonia . . . *Antonia!*" and I realized I was totally neglecting my best-friend responsibilities and uncrumpled the note in my lap.

What's on the agenda for project sainthood this month? I meant to ask you earlier. Sorry!

I gave her my sad you-don't-bring-me-flowers-anymore face, to which Maria responded by rolling her eyes. I slouched down to better hide my note-writing endeavors, which made me feel like a contortionist since I was sitting cross-legged in order to hide the fact that I was no longer wearing the awful Holy Angels uniform socks. Mom's efforts to unsluttify me were totally wasted. And yes, our school's full name is Holy Angels Catholic School for Girls, which is why we call it HA for short. Anyway, if the HA uniform patrol caught you without socks, they sent you home from school.

Very dangerous, the not-wearing-socks thing, but I liked to live on the edge.

Maria and I (that's Maria Romano, like the cheese) were sophomores, but she was a few months older than me, and already drove. Maria may have been blessed with long, dark, sleek hair, and was thin and as graceful as a gazelle and all, but she was also really shy. Except when she was with her best friend (me, of course). That's probably why it took her new lover-boy John Cronin so long to realize she was interested. Anyway, Maria was appropriately named after Saint Maria, the Patron Saint of Youth, and therefore beauty, life, and all that goes with youthfulness. We met in first grade back when we listened to whatever our mothers told us and spent all our free time building Lego submarines for the bathtub that really worked. This year marked our tenth anniversary of plaid skirts and Catholic school, but only our fourth without the male species.

The Discalced Carmelite Nuns who oversaw Holy Angels were okay with mixed company until sixth grade, and then they separated everybody in seventh, sending the girls off to the HA high school building and the boys off to Bishop Francis Academy next door, where Michael was a junior and where my destiny, Andy Rotellini, was also a junior. (*Discalced*, by the way, translates as "barefoot," which also means that technically my school was run by a group of women who call themselves the "Barefoot Nuns" even though I'd never seen any of them without shoes.) I supposed this separation of the sexes was to prevent us from engaging in Sins of the Flesh. Though the separation was not really necessary in my case, as I seemed to be rather unlucky at committing Sins of the Flesh.

Though I hoped to have reason to repent soon.

Glancing over, I saw that Maria was giving me a stare that said, "Hurry up and write back! Now!" so I scribbled my one-word response:

Figs

I crumpled the paper into a ball and tossed it into Maria's lap while uttering a quick prayer to St. Jude to prevent Sister Noella from catching my clandestine behavior. Jude is the Patron Saint of Desperate Situations and Hopeless Causes, a very useful all-purpose saint for school-day sneakiness among many other things, including aspiring to saintly glory, which at times feels like a hopeless cause.

"Nice," Maria whispered, showing approval for my current campaign, before pretending to take notes again.

Sister Noella had turned back around to lecture more about phenotypes, which have to do with how genes combine with our environment to determine bodily traits like curly hair, or, if you are a fruit fly, whether or not your wings work properly.

I am *not* some sort of religious freak, by the way, despite all my praying to saints and talking about them every other minute and expounding on their specializations and the fact that I know virtually everything there is to know about them, and I fully realize that sainthood is not exactly a normal ambition for a fifteen-year-old high school girl. And *no*, I am not interested in becoming a nun either. Saints, in my opinion, are simply the height of Catholic sophistication. Catholics are lucky to have a virtual Rolodex of thousands of women and men to call upon for help in very specific situations, and not just Jesus, who I see as basically an abyss of possibilities. With Jesus, you never know what you are going to get, if he was busy or just not interested in your little dilemma and ignoring you. But with the saints! At least with them you have everything narrowed down. Like, if I thought I might be coming down with strep, a little word to St. Etheldreda, Patron Saint Against Throat Diseases, and I'd be good to go. (I doubt Jesus would take the time to pay attention to a little sore throat—besides, he has bigger headaches to contend with, like saving the world one soul at a time and all that.)

Besides, as soon as I became the first living saint in history, I could show the world that sainthood was as cool as royalty. Like England and Monaco, Catholics have a vibrant royal past, the only difference being that all Catholic princes and princesses happened to be dead. And while I was aware that for two thousand years popes had been crowning people with this regal honor only after they had passed on to the great palace in the sky and often following some great personal trauma like being massacred by an angry mob or burning at the stake, I was not about to let a little detail like death get in my way.

To Become a Saint You Must Complete the Following:
1. The performance of two miracles.

   First miracle = beatification (which I like to think of as beautification).

   Second miracle = canonization (don't worry, it's *canon*, not *cannon*; there are no explosions).
2. Achieve great public renown for special abilities (which of course helps bring you to the attention of Rome, i.e., the Pope, who then bestows saintly glory on you for all eternity).

Technically, the third requirement is death, but I'd chosen to ignore that one for over eight years now (ignorance is bliss, I say!), ever since I turned seven and first decided I wanted to become a saint, which was also when my dad gave me my first Saint Diary for my birthday, inscribed with the words "To my little Antonia, the Patron Saint of Daddy's Heart." He died five weeks later in a car accident. Yeah, it was pretty devastating.

The very first letter I wrote to the Vatican? The very first saint I proposed? It was on March 1 just after we got home from the funeral. Gram helped me write the letter. It was very short.

Dear Holy Father the Pope,
    I hope you are well. Would you please make me the Patron Saint of Daddy's Heart? Thank you.

Blessings,
Antonia Lucia Labella

Sad and sweet and corny, I know.

Well, the Pope didn't go for it, unsympathetic jerk. He didn't even write back! We'd had the same pope, Gregory XVII, *FOREVER*, and now he was an old and crazy conservative and would be the death of the Catholic Church (or so some people said). He probably didn't even know I existed.

But, death aside, I firmly believed that if word got out among people my age about the possibilities of sainthood, there would be a rush of girls clamoring to cut in line. In front of *me*. Fox would probably have to host a reality show to accommodate everybody. Hundreds of thousands would turn out to audition.

I preferred to be in a line of one for sainthood, however.

This put the odds in my favor.

Maria was attempting to write another note but Sister

Noella kept turning her way, trying to give her the scary-nun-warning stare, but not really succeeding because Sister Noella was too sweet-natured. Sister Noella usually let us get away with *anything*. Maria and I both got straight A's and were actually first and second in our class, me being first and Maria being second, though we tried not to advertise this tidbit because it would seriously cramp our social life if people thought we were goody-goody smarty-pants.

We'd definitely rather be known as sexy-pants.

The clock read 10:52. Three more minutes of biology-lecture torture.

Maria was scribbling furiously. I was guessing it was a note to John. John was totally gorgeous and a senior at Bishop Francis. They smooched it up and then some after the October Holy Angels–Bishop Francis mixer, which our two schools alternated hosting once a month, you know, so we boys and girls could "mix" with one another. Regular smoothies, all of us. I didn't go because I wasn't allowed to go to dances until I turned sixteen, according to my mother, which, I often reminded her, was a full year *after* she started dating Dad back in the olden days.

Just over three months left and counting until February 14. I could already taste the freedom.

Lately Maria was alternately cloud-nine happy or all-out anxious about the status of John's feelings for her. Her feelings for him were never in question, however.

Another note flew into my lap.

Who's the patron saint of love anyway?

Aha. Maria was hoping for some intercession in the John-relationship project. Maybe it would stop her from being so moody about him.

Valentine, stupid! But technically he's not an official Catholic saint anymore — he's only a secular one. The Vatican denounced him in the sixties when they got all weird about love and sex and stuff (not that they weren't before). Said he never really existed and you can't have a saint that never existed. Can you believe that? St. Raphael is also technically about love, but he's no Valentine. Never really took off as a favorite.

The irony that the saint who shared my birthday got kicked out of the exclusive heavenly club to which I kept soliciting membership was not lost on me. But I tried not to take it as a bad sign for my prospects.

Maria mouthed "It figures" after reading my response, which really meant, of course the Catholic Church denounced the Patron Saint of Love since Catholics must pretend that anything to do with love and sexiness does not exist.

"What's next today?" I said under my breath.

"Gym," Maria said.

Ugh. Come through for me, Sebastian, I prayed.

When the bell finally rang and we uncurled our aching legs, Maria turned to me and said, "You know, Antonia, I think a Patron Saint of Figs is a great idea, and I totally know what you go through with your mother and those crazy fig trees you guys have in the yard. But seriously, don't you think we need to fill this Patron-Saint-of-Love vacancy? There's a major oversight if I've ever heard of one."

"I've thought of that," I said, stuffing books into my overflowing backpack, careful not to mangle my Saint Diary. "They'd never go for it, though, you know? It's the Catholic Church we're talking about, not an online dating service. Besides, I feel good about the figs proposal. The fig is practically the national fruit of Italy. I think this one is going to be the winner."

"Antonia," Maria said, giving me a knowing look, "if there was a real Patron Saint of Love, you know you'd be praying to him or her every day about you-know-who. And don't even try to tell me you wouldn't be scribbling devotions on all those scraps of paper you carry around, stuffing them in your book every five seconds. The page for the Saint of Love would surpass Anthony's in no time."

Hmmm. Maria had a point about the absent-love-saint problem. Though she should know not to blaspheme about St. Anthony, who would always be number one on my saint list.

"Come on, drama princess, we're going to be late for Mr. Sheehan," she said, giving a good push to the biology book I was still struggling to fit into my backpack.

Together we spilled into the hallway, a swirling sea of plaid and long hair and bare legs moving this way and that, lockers opening and slamming and laughter ringing everywhere. We merged into the stream of girls heading down the hall like a school of fish on its way to an important destination. But really we were only going to gym class, not at all critical in the grand scheme, and I wondered how it was possible to stand out in a place where everyone was made to look the same.

5

I Get Ready for My Monday Afternoon Shift and Reminisce About the First Time I Met Michael

Why is every day in my life a bad-hair day?" I asked my reflection in the bathroom mirror. This afternoon, like always, I'd returned home from school looking like I'd just walked out of a salon with a bad perm. I splashed my hair until it was almost soaking wet, trying to fix the tangled mess.

For some reason, I couldn't stop thinking about my encounter with Michael that morning. I felt sort of guilty about it. Had I been cold?

I wrapped a towel around my head, squeezing my way out of the bathroom and around all the clutter blocking the entrance to the bedroom that was barely big enough for the double bed where I slept, one chest of drawers, and the vanity set I inherited from my mother when I was eight. My statue of St. Anthony peeked up from the other side of my bed, almost as tall as the shelf that held seven years' worth of Saint Diaries. (Okay, so I also might have a free-standing saint statue in my room.)

I *did* have a nice window though, big enough so that I could crawl onto the fire escape outside.

The space above Labella's Market was not exactly a palace. The upstairs apartment where Gram, Mom, and I lived was *humble*. Meaning *really small*. The biggest room wasn't the family room or even any of the three bedrooms. It was the kitchen. The market didn't have its own, so our apartment served as cooking central for everything fresh sold at the store. When Dad's family immigrated from Italy, his father, my grandfather, built Labella's himself. To save money, he decided the family kitchen would not only be the place where everyone gathered for meals and on holidays but also provide the means for keeping the market stocked with all the homemade Italian specialties for which Mom's cooking had eventually made Labella's famous. Despite thirty years of business it had never occurred to anyone to renovate, so whoever worked at the store had an all-access pass to our kitchen. You never knew who you were going to see standing over the stove stirring the Italian cream for the zeppolis (filled Italian doughnuts) so it didn't burn or sipping an espresso at the table during a break. I guessed privacy wasn't a concern to Gram and Grandpa Labella. I always made sure I was fully dressed whenever I walked around the house.

All over the apartment were family portraits hung so close together on the walls you almost couldn't see the yellowed paper underneath. Most of the pictures were sepia-toned, some so faded in places that it looked like Great-grandma Amalia had no legs and the dress that Grandma Labella, Dad's mother, was wearing was shorter than my uniform skirt on a day I got out of the house without any mother-harassment. One of my favorites was of Grandpa Goglia, Gram's husband, in his police uniform, looking proud and handsome. My only sense of him was in sepia, since he died before I was born and I'd seen only this one portrait. The image closest to my door was a color photo of me and my three cousins—the daughters of my dad's sister, my aunt Silvia—Francesca, Concetta, and Veronica—back before they turned into mean girls. In the picture we were little—Veronica and I were four when it was taken—and wearing bathing suits, me in a one-piece and my cousin in a tiny bikini. Our chests were as flat as boards and our bellies stuck out. We were still in that blissful stage when the world thinks protruding tummies and nonexistent chests are adorable. Concetta and Francesca were acting the role of babysitters, watching over Veronica and me as we stood in the two-foot kiddie pool by the fig trees even though you could see our mothers in lawn chairs in the background.

Those were the days—before all the bad blood between our families poisoned everything.

Unfortunately, my cousins grew up to be three loud, mostly annoying, chubby (they're Italians, after all), boy-crazed girls always throwing themselves at the opposite sex in ways that made even me embarrassed. Of course, occasionally they were successful, which, I had to admit, was more than I could say for myself in the boy department. You'd think Veronica, Concetta, Francesca, and I all lived in the same house since they were always over at our apartment with their endless drama, acting like they owned it. At least one of them worked at the store every day.

"Antonia," my mother was always saying after the three of them left the apartment or the store, "if I ever catch you acting like those girls I'll never let you out of the house again!" I always wanted to answer, "But Ma! You don't let me out now as it is," but it was best to just nod my head. We had to tolerate them because they were family, she claimed. Though my mother and Aunt Silvia were barely able to tolerate each other.

When my father died, Aunt Silvia, Dad's sister, had assumed she would inherit Labella's and my mother would work for *her* to keep it in business. But Aunt Silvia couldn't even cook pasta from a box. And since Aunt Silvia's parents—my grandmother and grandfather on Dad's side—had passed on sole ownership of the store to my father, it was up to him to decide what happened to Labella's should he die. The rest is history: Dad left the family store to my mother even though she was originally a Goglia, honoring her role in turning it into the most famous Italian market around and ensuring that she and I would be taken care of. He only left 25 percent ownership to Aunt Silvia.

Aunt Silvia was livid, to put it mildly. She contested Dad's will and accused my mother of stealing what was rightfully hers. Relations between everyone had been strained ever since.

Veronica, though—she was the worst. We used to be like sisters before Dad died. The highlight of our day was if we somehow convinced Gram she should cook her famous Italian-style artichokes and then sit with us on the back steps deleafing them until we all got down to the delicious, juicy hearts. But between the fiasco with the store and the closer I became friends with Maria, it wasn't long before Veronica began acting like a bully.

My alarm clock read 3:50 p.m., which meant it was time to get ready for my shift. I unwrapped the towel from my hair, shaking the long, wet ringlets as they fell down my back, and threw on a black sweater. My tan skirt didn't seem to be anywhere. It wasn't in any of my drawers, and I began wondering if Gram had been in here and had stashed it under her bed. Or in the attic. Or perhaps in one of the kitchen cabinets. Things had been disappearing a lot lately, and Gram was my prime suspect. I grabbed a black skirt instead, one that I was pretty sure would hang below my knees, and dropped my uniform plaid in a heap on the floor. Yanking the other one up, I said a quick prayer of thanks to Paul the Hermit, the Patron Saint of Clothing and Weavers. The skirt fell to the middle of my shins.

For a woman worried about people seeing my legs, I found it ironic that my mother made everyone wear skirts to work at the market. I mean, half the time I was up on a ladder putting away bottles of olive oil on the high shelves in aisle 4 or taking something down for some old Italian guy from the neighborhood who was standing there, probably looking *up* my skirt. It was too gross to even imagine.

Though whenever my mother wasn't around, I'd just roll mine over at the waist to reach the middle of my thigh, just like I did with my uniform. You never knew who might walk into the store that you wanted to impress, you know?

Of course, I also never knew when Michael might stop by looking for something his mother wanted, which usually was also something that we stocked so high I needed the ladder to get it, at which point Michael would stand there below me while I searched for whatever his mother needed.

Waiting.

Watching.

Thinking what, I didn't really need to know.

With Michael, nothing ever felt innocent. I mean, the first thing I ever said to him the first time we spoke, all I did was ask one little question: "What are *you* looking at?"

Totally harmless, right?

I still couldn't decide if it was a mistake or a blessing — the fact that I spoke first, which also turned out to be the beginning of our, whatever you call it — friendship? Odd boy-girl relationship? It was at the beach in Narragansett two summers ago. Michael had a summer job lugging people's lounge chairs and umbrellas from the parking lot onto the sand for tips. I had a rare day off from the store and was trying to enjoy a day at the beach. I was outside the snack bar trying to crack a frozen Snickers bar with my teeth—making a fantastically gorgeous expression, I'm sure, as I chomped down on the corner—when I noticed someone staring at me with a smirk on his face.

First, I stopped gnawing and glared back, a don't-look-at-me-you-jerk glare. He didn't seem to care, though, and just kept on staring. I already felt self-conscious enough. It was my first summer wearing a two-piece bathing suit, since I was forbidden to show my stomach at the beach until I turned thirteen. (Don't ask where my mother got these rules. She just made them up as she went along.) I'd seen him before but I didn't know his name. He'd been in the store occasionally and I knew he went to Bishop Francis since he always wore the uniform.

So there I was, concentrating on my Snickers, trying to ignore him staring at me with what I now know is the Michael-girl-appreciation face (which is basically his permanent expression), and after what seemed like forever I finally got up the nerve to do something I never normally did with a boy I didn't already know.

I talked to him.

"What are *you* looking at?" I asked.

"Your legs," he answered, smiling and without skipping a beat in the Irish brogue that's so familiar to me now. His stare intensified.

My jaw dropped at his boldness, though I have to admit I'd felt a kernel of relief that he didn't say something like "I'm watching your bizarre wolflike attack on that candy bar" instead.

"You heard me," he said as if I'd answered him, when really I just stood there speechless.

"Um, what . . ." I said, which he took as an invitation to continue the conversation.

"I'm looking at your legs."

"Excuse me?"

"You asked me what I was looking at and I answered you."

"Excuse me?" Okay, I got repetitive.

"Would you prefer I lie to you?"

"No. I mean, yes! I mean, I can't believe you just said that! It's totally inappropriate."

Question: Could I have sounded more like my mother in this moment?

Answer: No.

"They're nice."

"What?" I asked next, still playing the role of confused girl.

"Your legs are nice."

My cheeks were on fire at this point, matching my new red gingham bikini, which I began to wish was cut more in the style of a spacesuit.

"My name is Michael," he said, his eyes rising to meet mine, which, I admit, almost made me melt on the spot despite all his unnerving forward behavior. They were a bright greenish blue, their color seeming to change back and forth with the glimmer of the sun. He was good-looking, I decided. This made my heart pound so hard that I worried he might hear.

"Are you going to tell me your name?" His eyes were huge and unblinking. I couldn't look away.

My mouth opened but nothing came out.

"You want me to guess, then?" He was grinning now, which made me notice that he also had a nice smile.

"No. I'm not telling you my name," I said, finally. "You're kind of rude, you know."

He took this response as a challenge.

"Tanisha?"

"No."

"October?"

"That's not a name, it's a month," I said, letting my guard down a little. A laugh escaped despite my better judgment.

"I once knew a girl named October."

"I bet you did," I said, smirking.

"Bronwyn! Your name is Bronwyn."

"I can't believe you guessed right," I said, laughing hard now.

Somehow our conversation continued for hours that day and throughout the rest of that summer. We were a weird pair when you considered that I was as pure as the driven snow and Michael was more like the snow after it spent a week on the city streets. We became inseparable, with Michael even hanging out after curfew by climbing up the fire escape outside my bedroom and talking to me through the window. But we stopped being inseparable the day he tried to kiss me behind the bathhouses and I got really mad because:

(a) I'd thought we were just friends.

(b) It wasn't as if he'd been leaving out details about his escapades with, like, every girl in the grade above mine at Holy Angels.

(c) He knew I liked somebody else even if that somebody didn't ever give me the time of day.

Who did he think I was anyway? Just another girl who fell for the accent and his ridiculous one-liners?

No way. I was not going to be one of *those* girls. And I conveyed this to him the second I realized he was about to kiss me, but not so much in words and more in the way that I turned around and ran in the other direction and then stopped hanging out with him from that day forward because I was petrified he'd try to kiss me again.

He didn't.

The red glare of the clock told me it was already 3:58, so I pushed all thoughts of Michael McGinnis out of my head. I took one last glance in the mirror and rubbed St. Anthony's halo for luck out of habit before grabbing my book bag and racing out of my bedroom to the back stairway that led down to the market. At the top of the steps I paused, uttering a quick prayer to Leonard of Noblac, the Patron Saint of Grocers and an important saint if your family happened to own a market.

O St. Leonard of Noblac, please let everyone get along tonight during my shift, and don't let Francesca be a pain in everyone's butt, especially my mother's, because then she always makes me the one to deal with Francesca's messes and I really hate that. And if you could inspire Andy Rotellini's mother to need a rare imported olive oil, or perhaps a spinach pie, or really anything at all that would send her hottie son to Labella's this evening while I'm working, I'd be forever grateful. Thank you, St. Leonard, for your intercession in this matter.

Descending the stairs one at a time, I embarked on yet another afternoon at Labella's Market, where you could buy "The Finest, Freshest Homemade Pasta in all Rhode Island." At least, that's what the sign in the window said.

6

The Love of My Life, Andy Rotellini, Visits the Store and I Am Witness to a Major Miracle

Antonia! Who died?" My mother looked up from the "Today's Specials" chalkboard to give my outfit the once-over. She was carefully erasing the stuff that was already sold out, which included every kind of pasta except the fresh, hand-cut linguini. It was looking rather lonely in the display fridge.

"What are you talking about, Ma?" I said, squeezing behind her ample frame so I could shove my backpack behind the counter. I picked up the "To Do" notebook by the old-fashioned cash register. There was a page with my name and today's date at the top.

For Antonia, November 14, 4 p.m.
—stock all new produce
—organize storeroom
—home deliveries: Mrs. Bevalaqua, Mr. Romanelli

"Hi, Gram," I said, peeking around the door frame to the back office. She stopped reading her tabloid long enough to blow me a kiss. "Love you, too," I said, and headed back out front.

"Where's Frankie today?" Francesca hated that nickname from when we were kids, so I tried to use it often when I thought she might be around.

"She called in sick."

Score one for the good St. Leonard, I thought to myself, but said out loud, "That's too bad, I hope she gets better soon."

"You look like you're going to a funeral, wearing all black like that, Antonia."

"Look who's talking, Ma," I said, wedging past her again and pinching the sleeve of her black blouse.

"I have no idea what you mean," my mother said as if she didn't really know.

Right.

"Whatever, Ma," I called back as I made my way around the tower of imported canned San Marzano tomatoes that I'd spent all Saturday afternoon stacking.

My mother still dressed like a widow, all in black, at church, in the market, everywhere she went. I usually avoided the subject since she was sensitive about it, but today I couldn't help myself. Dad died eight years ago, but she still acted like it was yesterday. I couldn't decide if this was sad or ridiculous or a bit of both. I mean, we all missed him and it had been difficult getting used to life without him, but wearing black from head to toe didn't exactly help Mom to move on, and it certainly didn't say "Ask me out" to any potential suitors either. It was kind of gross to think about my mother dating, but I had to admit that some of the men who came into the store flirted with her. She didn't seem to notice, though.

She wore the widow's black like a suit of protective armor.

I flipped the light on in the storeroom, and propped the door open with a big bag of rice. The boxes from the new shipment of vegetables and fruits were piled high in the back corner—eggplant, tomatoes, broccoli, apples from the local orchard. It would take at least two hours to put everything out into the baskets and the open-air refrigerator that lined the produce aisle, which led me to wonder if, when I was named the first living saint in Catholic history, I was still going to have to arrange tomatoes and ring up spinach pies. Though I couldn't imagine *not* working at the market, since I also couldn't remember a time when it hadn't been a part of my life.

I heaved the boxes marked "McIntosh" and "Tomatoes on the vine" onto a dolly and maneuvered it out the door and over to the produce aisle. The tomatoes smelled good. As soon as I opened the first box I grabbed one off the top and bit into it, careful not to let the juice drip onto the floor, or, worse, down my sweater. I began emptying the clusters onto the "Tomatoes, 2.99 per lb." display with my free hand. There were a few perks working at the family market, eating all the yummy food being number one.

"Your friend Michael was here about a half hour ago, Antonia," Gram said, shuffling her way into view. "You just missed him. I meant to mention it before, but I don't know what happened. I should have written it down. He asked for manicotti, but I think he was really looking for you," she said, starting to giggle. "Don't worry, I won't say anything to your mother."

"Um, thanks, Gram," I said, watching as she shuffled back out of sight. I noticed she was wearing bedroom slippers and wondered if she couldn't find her shoes.

The bell by the front door jingled, signaling a customer's arrival, and several voices began speaking at once. Taking another bite out of my tomato, I stopped stocking and listened.

"How nice to see you, Nicoletta," my mother said in her singsongy, welcome-to-Labella's voice, and I gasped, almost choking on the little tomato seeds that flew down the back of my throat. I tried not to cough.

"Nice to see you, too, Amalia," said the mystery woman . . .

. . . who totally sounded like . . .

"You remember my son, of course."

Son? Did she say "son"? Was it possible *he* was *here*?

"How are you, Andrew?"

"I'm fine, Mrs. Labella," said a deep male voice. I crouched down to see through the space between the vegetable baskets and the rows of imported pasta on the other side of the aisle, which gave me a perfect view of the counter . . . and . . .

OHMIGOSH. It was definitely HIM. THE LOVE OF MY LIFE WAS IN THE MARKET. Andy Rotellini was in the store shopping with his mother! St. Leonard was on a roll today. I already couldn't wait to tell Maria that Andy was virtually in my room on my bed! Well, technically, he was underneath my room and my bed, but still. From my discreet viewing window I could also confirm that, yes, Andy was still as tall, dark, and gorgeous as I remembered. If he hadn't been talking, right at that very moment, to both his mother and mine, it would've been hard to stop myself from going right up to him and running my hand through his soft, curly hair and finding out if that perfect olive skin felt as good as it looked. And those eyes! How could I keep myself from staring into those big brown pools of perfection, hoping that he might grace me with that brilliant smile I'd loved from the moment I'd first seen it?

Though he didn't smile often. Andy was a bit of a brooder, but I didn't care.

He could brood with me any day.

The first time I saw Andy he was playing baseball in the park down the street. It was just before I started ninth grade at HA, one of the last days of summer. I stood outside the fence watching him pitch. I couldn't take my eyes off him. It was love at first sight. Well, at least on my end. I found out later that his family had moved in a few blocks away on Atwells Avenue, just a quick walk from the market. His mother came into the store all the time for groceries, spinach pies, and occasionally some pasta. Not that I kept track. But usually *without* her son.

Can you believe that Andy Rotellini was practically sitting on my bed making out with me? At least in my imagination?

Breathe, Antonia.

"Why don't you come into the back and we'll sit and talk," my mother was saying to Mrs. Rotellini and Andy. "Antonia? Where are you? I need you to come watch the register, please."

"Oww," I exclaimed, so startled when she outed me that I banged my head on the wooden shelf above the vegetable basket.

"Antonia?"

"I'm coming, I'm coming," I said, throwing my half-eaten tomato into the empty box. I quickly rolled up my skirt, took a deep breath, and walked down the aisle mustering as much poise and sexiness as a nervous girl about to see her beloved could.

"Oh, *hi*, Mrs. Rotellini," I said in my best nonchalant voice, smiling my biggest smile, acting like I was surprised to see her.

"Hello, Antonia," she said without much interest, clearly unaware that she was talking to her future daughter-in-law.

"Hi, Andy," I added, worrying that with just two words he'd be able to detect my eagerness and the fact that I was practically drooling on behalf of his perfect beauty.

"Hey," he answered, nodding.

Okay. Andy wasn't a man of many words. But so what? He was also with his mother, so it wasn't like we were in the best situation for a major conversation, much less any flirting. I waited for him to say something else but he didn't and my mother was already shepherding everyone into the back room, which I thought was odd, but I wasn't about to complain.

Because ANDY ROTELLINI WAS IN THE MARKET!

Maybe I'll catch him on the way out, I thought and reached under the counter to retrieve my backpack to review for biology, resisting the urge to scribble away more petitions in my Saint Diary. And while Mom conversed with my future husband about who knows what, I found out why studying genetics could be useful. By reading the assigned chapter, I learned that when Andy and I procreated someday we would have children with curly hair because curly hair is a dominant-gene trait, with a capital C. I played with one of my long twists out of habit, which then made me wonder if when the Vatican made me a saint they would make me cut my hair short. This would be unfortunate. I'd tried short hair in the past and it made me look like a poodle, and I doubted Andy would go for a girl who looked like a poodle.

It was difficult to concentrate with Andy, his mother, and my mother having a private discussion so close by. The clock said five p.m. and I still had to put out the rest of the produce, organize the storeroom, and handle Mrs. Bevalaqua's delivery, and Mr. Romanelli's, too. It would be a long night, since grocery delivery was never a matter of leaving orders and taking off. With Mrs. B I always unpacked everything and did all the dishes, and then with Mr. Romanelli, we sat and looked at pictures of his kids and grandkids every time I visited. He never remembered that I'd looked through his photo albums, like, a gazillion times now.

The bell attached to the door jingled again. I glanced up and all thoughts of Andy Rotellini in the back room disappeared in an instant. (Well, almost all of them.) I watched, open-mouthed, as our new customer ambled slowly, carefully, toward the counter, her gray hair pinned up neatly in a bun, elegant dress gloves covering her delicate hands.

"Hello, Antonia," she said, her eyes sparkling, and that familiar, warm smile spreading wide across her face.

"Mrs. Bevalaqua! You're . . . you're . . ." I said, trying to find the words. It wasn't that I was surprised to see Mrs. Bevalaqua—she'd occasionally rolled her way down to the store on her own in the past. But, it was just, her entrance, I mean, it was almost, I don't know . . .

A miracle?

She was . . . *walking*.

No. It wasn't possible. I rubbed my eyes, trying to clear whatever was making me see this illusion. But the illusion didn't go away.

It was real.

Mrs. Bevalaqua was walking!

"St. Sebastian," I whispered, conjuring with wonder that familiar golden image of the boy with all the arrows in my mind. "Did you do this, Sebastian? *Did you?*" I asked, my eyes glancing toward heaven.

"What was that, honey?" Mrs. Bevalaqua asked when she arrived at the register.

"Nothing," I said, blinking away tears. I walked out from behind the counter to take in the vision that was Mrs. Bevalaqua, standing before me. "Mom," I called out, no longer concerned about who my mother was talking to or what they might be discussing. "Mom? Gram? I think you'd better come out here! There's someone here to see us!"

"It's been so strange, Antonia." Mrs. Bevalaqua's voice was matter-of-fact, as if old women confined for decades to wheelchairs got up and walked every day. "Ever since you gave me that kiss on the cheek this morning—it made my toes start tingling and then my legs, and, well, I won't bore you with all the details, but here I am. Don't just stand there now. I won't break, I don't think."

"I'm sure you won't," I said, throwing my arms around her, and thinking, as we stood there together, that the world was indeed a miraculous place.

7

ANDY IS NOWHERE TO BE FOUND, AND SEVEN ANGELS GUARD US FROM PREDATORY BOYS IN THE HA–BISHOP FRANCIS PARKING LOT

The week passed quickly and soon it was Friday morning, the day before the great fig-tree burying. I was on my way to meet Maria by her car in the parking lot, near the big marble angel statue of St. Gabriel. There were seven statues in all, each representing the seven archangels—Michael, Gabriel, Raphael, Uriel, Raguel, Sariel, and even the fallen Lucifer—forming a kind of protective wall between HA and Bishop Francis, as if the nuns who founded our school were trying to ward off the boys with God's army.

But no army, godly or otherwise, could scare me at the moment. I was on cloud nine about the week's two biggest events.

The whole neighborhood was buzzing about Mrs. Bevalaqua's miraculous healing. She'd been to visit the store again last night, at which point Mom, Gram, Mrs. B, and I celebrated her cure with tiny glasses of limoncello. Though

Mrs. B kept insisting on toasting *me*. For some reason she associated that peck on the cheek with the beginning of her recovery. I kept telling her that if we were going to toast anybody it should be St. Sebastian, since he was the man to thank for the miracle. But Mrs. B wouldn't hear of it and Mom kept shushing me and saying I needed to stop contradicting my elders.

Second only to Mrs. Bevalaqua's recovery was the thrilling news that Mom had hired Andy Rotellini as a stock boy (!!!), proving, yet again, that the saints were making miracles happen all the time.

"Antonia, you need a serious uniform adjustment," Maria said the second I arrived. She was staring at my kneesocks. As usual, Maria was the picture of Catholic Girl Hotness and probably didn't even realize it. No wonder so many guys were in love with her. Little did they know we were, like, the last two surviving virgins at Holy Angels.

"Oh, right, thanks," I said, kicking off my loafers so I could take off my socks. "Mom's been giving me such a hard time about the uniform lately. She's been lurking by the door every morning, waiting to pounce. Gram thinks it's hilarious."

"Your grandmother would probably let you out naked if your mom wasn't around," Maria said, laughing.

"Yeah. Gram's a little crazy."

"A little? She hid a coffeepot in your underwear drawer last week."

"She just put it down and forgot about it," I said in Gram's defense.

"In your underwear drawer? Why did she have a coffeepot in your room anyway?"

"I really don't know, Maria," I said, "but can we change the subject to more important topics? Like the fact that aside from Miraculous Monday, there have been zero Andy Rotellini sightings and I am too scared to ask my mother what his start date is because I don't want her to get suspicious. It's been three whole days."

"Don't worry. Soon you'll be seeing Andy on a regular basis."

"I know," I said dreamily. "But when? And can I just say one more time that he looked so hot Monday night that I thought I might die."

"I am willing to listen as many times as you need to tell me." Maria is truly the best kind of best friend.

"Andy had on his white Bishop Francis oxford, which totally set off his gorgeous, dark skin, and I couldn't tear my eyes away. Well, except to notice how good his butt looked in the jeans he was wearing. And, he was standing right underneath my bed, Maria. If only I could have gotten him upstairs," I added, wistful. "Monday night marked the first time that Andy and I moved beyond exchanging mutual 'heys.' "

"An important occasion, I agree," Maria said.

Mrs. Bevalaqua couldn't have picked a better moment to get miraculously cured and show up at the market.

Once everyone heard me yelling and came to see what the fuss was about, it got a little chaotic with all the excitement and celebrating. Ma and Mrs. Rotellini were taking turns hugging Mrs. B and saying loud prayers of thanks to Jesus (wrong guy if you asked me—Sebastian was clearly the miracle worker here), and then Mom pulled out a bottle of brandy. This allowed Andy and me the opportunity for meaningful conversation, since no one was offering us any brandy.

"Hey, Antonia," he'd said in his sexy voice. "Where do I find the tomatoes that come in the yellow cans?"

"The San Marzanos, you mean?" My voice was ever so calm. But I have to add: I thought it was a little strange that Andy was worried about tomatoes when we were, at that very moment, witnessing what might be the greatest miracle of the twenty-first century, not to mention the fact that this was his first time alone with the future love of his life: me.

Meanwhile, brandy snifters were clinking in the background. Then Andy began walking toward me, at which point I thought to myself, NOW! KISS ME NOW OUT OF JOY FOR MRS. B! QUICK, while Ma and everyone are getting DRUNK!

He didn't, though. Instead he said, "Yeah, I guess. Yeah, that's what I want. My mother's making a sauce. How many, do you think? I don't really want to bother her right now." He gestured at the brandy-sniffing foursome to explain his reluctance before turning his giant brown eyes back to me.

"Two of the big cans or three of the smaller ones," I answered, dazzled by his stare but still confused why we were talking about groceries when there were so many other interesting things happening around us. "There is a huge tower of San Marzanos in the far-right aisle, on the left, toward the middle. You can't miss them." Of course, inside I was still screaming, KISS ME! KISS ME! DO SOMETHING ROMANTIC FOR ST. JUDE'S SAKE!

"Great, thanks," Andy said, walking away, luckily not having heard a word of anything I was thinking. He seemed totally unmoved by the lightning storm of emotion behind us. Maybe Andy was the quiet, silent type on the surface, but deep and passionate underneath?

"Earth to Antonia," Maria said, snapping me out of my daydream. "Let's figure out how you can take advantage of the serendipitous opportunity your mother just handed you by hiring Andy."

As Maria speculated that Andy Rotellini was sure to fall in love with me in aisle 3, where the light falls in such a way that it gives everyone an angelic glow, and soon we would be going on double dates with her and John, out of the corner of my eye I noticed Hilary, Angela, and Lila a few cars away, drooling over the two hockey-player seniors from Bishop Francis that were chatting them up. When they saw me watching, they paused long enough to smile and wave, but soon turned their full attention back to the guys. Girls at HA died for Bishop Francis hockey players. Angela and Lila were both cheerleaders, and I was sure, at the moment, they were envisioning themselves proudly wearing letter jackets to the season opener this coming weekend. I would of course miss the game because of the fig-tree-burying extravaganza. Some HA girls, like Angela and Lila, were what Maria and I called "Seasonal." Well, really they were *Aspiring* Seasonals.

Definition of a "Seasonal" Catholic Schoolgirl

Seasonal girls date guys according to the current sports season. For example, you date the soccer star during soccer season, the hockey star during the winter, the best baseball pitcher during spring. Then you always have a game to go to, a guy to root for, a letter jacket to wear with the appropriate star-player-guy's name on it while you're oohing and aahing him in the stands. Some girls take it even further and try to find a guy who will cover them for more than one season, meaning he's a superathlete and plays both soccer and hockey, or football and baseball (but then those winter months are really a drag).

I know what you are thinking: not very feminist of us to be revolving our love lives around our ability to say "Go, sweetie!" from the sidelines at a game, but hey, don't blame me. I didn't make the rules. I'm just the messenger.

I suspected that Lila had better karma for success in the Seasonal Dating department since Angela had the misfortune of being named after the Patron Saint *Against* Sexual Temptation, which was almost as bad as being named after the Patron Saint of Teenage Purity. Of course, with my record I'd be lucky to date a guy on the chess team. Maybe I should try being *Off* Seasonal, and go after the guy *before* the season started so there would be less competition. Like now, when we were a full two seasons before baseball, Andy's sport. When the season began he would become far more desirable and every girl I knew would be watching him pitch at games, and the team would start wearing those ugly satin baseball jackets that all the girls dream of snagging.

"What's on your mind? I can tell you're scheming," Maria asked, studying my face.

"Well," I said, leaning against the hood of Maria's old blue Honda, trying to pull off a casual yet sexy look but wondering if I looked as uncomfortable as I really felt against the cold metal, "I was just thinking that I have a better chance of getting Andy now, while baseball season is a distant memory in our pretty classmates' heads. Though, with my luck, Andy will start dating some girl this weekend, while I'm busy burying the fig trees."

"You know I'll help with the burying, so that should give you at least some socializing time," Maria said. She helped with the figs every year.

"It's always nice to have the company," I said, grateful. "And speaking of company, why is it that I am perfectly good at attracting girl company, all of our neighbors whenever they have a problem they need fixing, and even little boys when there's a skinned elbow in need of attention. But Andy—nowhere to be found!"

"Maybe we need to make you look more . . . *available*," Maria said, reaching out and deftly undoing the top two buttons of my oxford, then cocking her head to observe the effect. "That's much better. Just because your mother locks you in at night doesn't mean we can't find other ways of getting Andy to notice how totally gorgeous you are."

I played with the delicate filigree necklace I always wore, visible now that my oxford was open at the neck. Mom gave it to me for my confirmation—the day I officially became an adult member of the Catholic Church and therefore could also, someday in the future, marry Andy Rotellini at Our Lady of Loreto.

"Hey, before I forget, I brought the clothes you left at my house last week. They're somewhere in back," Maria said, opening the passenger door of her car.

"Oh, yeah, thanks," I said, folding down the front seat to search for my stuff. One of the only social things I was allowed to do was sleep over at Maria's. We had big plans coming up for the December Holy Angels–Bishop Francis Winter Formal. The big plans being that I was actually going to go by way of Maria's house.

"Look out, Antonia. Here comes your favorite Bishop Francis admirer," Maria sang from her perch on the front of her car, where she'd been observing the scene in the parking lot.

Somewhere in my before-school brain-fog it registered that she meant that Michael, not Andy, was on his way over. I fought the urge to cower in the backseat.

"He's approaching. Patrick McMahon is with him. They are, let's see, about ten cars away but talking to every girl in between, so you've got some time to make a decision," Maria narrated. Her loafers were banging against the side of her car. "What do you want me to do here, lover-girl?"

"Don't call me lover-girl," I said from the backseat, where I was now sitting, bag of clothes on my lap.

"But you kind of are lover-girl when it comes to Michael McGinnis. He is so still crushing on you and you obviously have some strange fixation for him. You are *always* talking about him, Antonia."

"We're just friends," I said, with more confidence than I actually felt. Inside I wasn't entirely sure what Michael and I were exactly. "Besides, Michael crushes on *everybody*."

"If you just like him as a friend, Antonia, then why are you hiding in my car?"

"I can't decide if I feel like talking to him right now, okay?" I sighed.

Through the car's front window I could see Michael walking toward us, his blue Bishop Francis uniform tie hanging loose, shirt half out, looking as disheveled as the dark, wavy brown hair that fell around his face in messy layers. If Michael had a superpower, it would be the ability to home in on my location no matter where I hid. He looked right past Maria into the car where I was sitting. Ever since the day we met, something about Michael's stare always made me wish I was wearing a huge sweatshirt and baggy, unflattering pants. I knew this was not a normal reaction to someone who also happened to be the guy with whom half your school was trying to lock lips despite the fact that he didn't even play a sport. Maybe it was his Irish brogue that got him all the girls. It *was* pretty charming. Or maybe his eyes? Whatever it was, *I* was not falling for it. If Michael ever tried to kiss me again, not that he would and definitely not that I would want him to, I would run the other way just like last time, because though a kiss may be just a kiss for Michael, I wanted my first kiss to be perfect and NOT with the kissing bandit of Bishop Francis Academy for Boys.

Besides, I was saving myself for Andy Rotellini.

"You're obsessing over him, aren't you, Antonia?"

"Who, Andy?"

"Nooooo," Maria said. "Your 'friend.' "

"I am not," I lied, and said a quick prayer in my head to Vitus, Patron Saint Against Animal Attacks, about turning Michael's attention in another direction since he practically *was* an animal when it came to girls. At least, that's what I'd heard. "I was just petitioning St. Jude about my fig proposal at the Vatican." Why lie only once when you were on a roll? "And being thankful about Mrs. Bevalaqua's miraculous recovery," I added for good measure.

"More like you were just praying to Jude about the hopeless cause that would be *you* not obsessing about Michael McGinnis."

"If you don't stop harassing me about him, I'm going to tell John about how last year you drew hearts all over your notebooks and filled them with 'Maria loves John,' like you were still in elementary school."

"You wouldn't do that to your best friend."

"Just try me."

"Uh-ho! Your cousins to the rescue, baby." Maria was back to her play-by-play. "Veronica and Concetta have intercepted Michael and Patrick two cars away and are engaged in some heavy flirting," she informed me. "And damn! Veronica's got her skirt hiked up as high as that cheesy banana-clip hairdo she always wears. That girl needs to learn that hair spray and teasing is not attractive."

Veronica was in our class and Concetta was one year ahead of us—a junior.

A wave of relief washed over me. But then I couldn't help wondering if either of the Italian wonder twins were somehow involved with Michael. Not that I cared. I was just curious.

"Hey, Maria," I said, finally emerging from her backseat. "Let's get out of here before they come over. I've got to finish an essay anyway."

"Okay, lover-girl."

"Stop calling me that!"

"All right, let's go," she said, hopping off the front of her car and linking her arm through mine.

We passed Michael, Patrick, and my two cousins as we crossed the threshold of angels at the edge of the parking lot. Even though I stared straight ahead I could feel Michael's eyes on me, and my cheeks began to burn.

8

Sister Mary Margaret Fails to Teach Us Anything, and Veronica and I Have a Public Spat

P lease open your texts and read quietly," Sister Mary Margaret said, looking up from the open book on her desk, her tone stern. Unlike Sister Noella, Sister Mary Margaret wore the old-fashioned nun's habit, the *Sound of Music* kind with the stiff white frame that left only a tiny oval window for the face and covered everything else — ears, hair, and neck.

We were reading *The Great Gatsby* in class, *literally*. Sister Mary Margaret didn't actually teach. We spent almost all our time "reading quietly," and when Sister Mary Margaret thought we'd had enough "reading quietly," she gave us a test on whatever book we'd spent zero minutes discussing.

Lila Delman (of the Lila, Angela, Hilary trio) was trying to get my attention — never a good idea with Sister Mary Margaret watching. Lila always sat next to me whenever I had class without Maria. "Hey, Antonia," she was whispering. "Antonia . . ."

I gave Lila the we're-going-to-get-in-trouble-if-we're-not-careful stare.

Apparently, Lila had trouble understanding my signal. Soon she was leaning toward me, trying to start a conversation, her perky blond hair swinging forward. "So can you hang out in the parking lot today after school? Hilary, Angela, and I met these totally hot guys from the hockey team and they said they'd see us there today and we could share the wealth . . ."

"Can't do it," I'd already written on one of the slips I kept in my bag for saint petitions, holding it up so Lila could read it from her desk.

Plans with Maria. Sorry. Love 2 next time!

Friday was my one afternoon off from working at the store.

"Maria could come too if she wanted . . . though she might not be interested since, well, she's dating that senior guy at Bishop Francis, isn't she?"

Lila was still talking when Sister Mary Margaret suddenly yelled, "Was there something confusing about my request that you open your books and read quietly?" which silenced Lila midsentence, and together as a class we gave the expected response . . .

"No, Sister Mary Margaret," we said in unison, making sure to draw out each syllable clearly.

. . . and which ended any attempt of Lila's to continue our conversation. Everyone went back to *The Great Gatsby*, or whatever else they were doing before the interruption: homework for another class, writing notes to friends and loved ones, doodling, reading trashy romance novels, or, in my case, reflecting about the fact that it was now seventeen days since I'd sent the fig proposal to the Vatican.

I'd suggested a grand total of 103 specialties so far—all rejected, with the Patron Saint of Figs and Fig Trees clocking in at number 104. That's one saint specialization a month, every month, for almost nine years. Some people would've gotten discouraged already. But not me. I was nothing if not persistent. Besides, I was confident that soon the Vatican would take notice of at least one of my ideas. At least *mine* were always practical, unlike some specializations that were pretty ridiculous. For example, there are official saints for rheumatoid chorea (I don't even know what that is), pewterers, which I think are people who make pewter objects (??), bachelors (though not *bachelorettes*, interestingly enough), and disappointing children (whether this means warding against letting down your offspring or a child who is less than satisfying, I am not quite sure). All these in addition to saints for beekeeping, bartending, unattractive people, cattle, and, all kidding aside, a separate specialty for diseased cattle (perhaps for mad cow?), feet problems, plague, not to mention spelunking (for you nonoutdoorsy types, that's caving). There are even saints for Belgian and Spanish *air crews*—you know, pilots and airline attendants. But, bizarrely enough, there *isn't* a Patron Saint of Gelato! (I tried that one when I was nine.) Or Secret Keeping! (I floated that one just last month after Gram overheard me talk about Andy to Maria and I was afraid she might spill the beans.) And, of course, figs. No Patron Saint of Figs! Not yet, at least.

Waiting is the worst.

After staring at page 96 for ten straight minutes, I decided to organize the most recent petitions in my Saint Diary, including the one I wrote last period to St. Jude about kissing.

Everyone I knew had, at the very least, kissed someone. I was probably the only girl at Holy Angels who'd still never gotten any tongue. Talk about having a reason to pray to St. Jude. I could be the poster child for the Hopeless Cause when it came to kissing.

Dear St. Jude:

O Patron Saint of Desperate Situations and Hopeless Causes, I am indeed desperate and I know you can help. All I want is a little kiss. I know that wanting to be kissed is probably not something you think a good virgin Catholic like me should be asking for, but believe me, a little kiss from Andy isn't even going to make a dent in my purity, I'm oh-so-untouched. So if you are at all worried about my Virginity, please stop, and if you could turn the attention of the love of my life my way, I'll be eternally grateful.

Actually, if you could turn his lips in my direction specifically, that would be best. Thank you, St. Jude, for your intercession in this matter.

"Antonia, what *are* you going on about?" Lila was staring at me, her eyebrows raised, her voice *so* not a whisper.

I froze. Had I read my petition to Jude out loud?

What was WRONG with me?

It took only one innocent question from Lila to get all sixteen pairs of eyes in Sister Mary Margaret's American lit class, including my cousin Veronica's, on me. People were always looking for excuses to break up the daily boredom.

"Um, I'll tell you later, okay?" I pleaded, my voice quiet.

"Antonia, did you have something you wanted to tell us?" Sister Mary Margaret piped up from her desk, frowning, her forehead a mass of wrinkles along the edge of her nun's habit.

"I was just commenting to myself about the story," I began, praying that Lila had not really heard all that stuff I was asking St. Jude about my aspirations to kiss Andy Rotellini. "I guess I got so caught up in the book I forgot where I was and spoke my thoughts out loud. Sorry."

"And those thoughts were what? Why don't you share with the class? Tell us what you think of *The Great Gatsby*." Her voice was skeptical.

"Sorry," Lila mouthed, her pale skin flushing red.

"Why don't you tell us, Toni," Veronica snickered, using the nickname from my childhood that she knew I hated. Just hearing her nasally voice and that thick Rhode Island Italian accent made my body tense.

I shot Veronica—who was smiling cruelly—an evil look for two reasons. First, *no one* called me Toni. I was not a boy and I did *not* do nicknames. When I was a little girl and my father was still alive he used to say I had a beautiful name, which is why he and Mom gave it to me, and therefore there was no reason to shorten it. Like I mentioned before, really I am Antonia *Lucia*, just like Mom is Amalia Lucia and Gram is Editta Lucia—but I leave it at Antonia.

Second, Veronica was just plain wicked and would love to see me humiliated in front of the class. St. Veronica may be the Patron Saint of Laundry Workers (and given the marinara stain from lunch on Veronica's white oxford, she could stand to do a little washing), but it would be more true to form if my cousin's name saint was the Patron of Hurtful Gossip or of Mean Remarks or even of People With Nasty Souls.

"Antonia?" Sister Mary Margaret pressed, perhaps awakened by the strange sight of people in her class paying attention.

"It was me that was talking, Sister Mary Margaret, not Antonia . . . *really* . . ." Lila started babbling, but one look from Sister Mary Margaret silenced her.

"I was talking to Antonia. Is your name Antonia?"

"No, Sister," Lila said.

"I was just saying to *myself*," I said finally, "that if Gatsby puts up with any more agita—that's Italian slang for aggravation—from Daisy, then he's likely to become a saint, or he should at least consider praying to St. Rose, the Patron Saint Against Vanity, because Daisy really has some problems in that area."

Right then the bell rang and I was saved from any further public trials.

"Tomorrow we'll continue reading," Sister Mary Margaret said, but her redundant directive was lost in the din of an entire class of girls already on the move, getting out of seats, slamming books shut, packing up, the little exchange between Veronica, Sister, Lila, and me already forgotten. I felt thankful for small miracles like bells that end class with perfect timing and made a mental note that there should be a Patron Saint of Quick Thinking.

"I'm *soooo* sorry about that, Antonia," Lila said, her blue eyes apologetic.

"No worries."

"But now that we *can* talk . . . what *were* you saying anyway? I definitely heard something about kissing and the name Andy," she said, her face turning from apologetic to curious. "Did you mean Andy Rotellini? Because if you did I don't blame you. He's *so* cute."

"Maybe I did," I whispered, wondering if it might not be such a big deal to confess my love interests to more friends than just Maria. "Have you ever seen him pitch a game? He looks so good in his uniform and a baseball hat."

"Guys always look good in baseball hats, don't they?"

"They *do* do," I said, zipping up my bag, but not before Lila got a glimpse of what I'd been packing away.

"What's that big red book you're always carrying around anyway?"

My Saint Diary was not something I was ready to share, so I just told Lila it was for a project I was working on, which is also when I noticed Veronica standing nearby.

"You know I don't like it when people call me Toni," I said, unable to mask my anger.

"Well, *sorry*," Veronica said in a mocking tone. "God. I was just kidding around. You're so sensitive. You really *are* the baby of the family, aren't you? Maybe that's why you couldn't deal with Michael . . ."

"Veronica," I said, cutting her off, confused why she'd know to bring up Michael. "You may think I'm a baby, but you should really spend some time thinking about why the only person willing to hang out with you at HA is your sister."

"Does she mean Michael McGinnis?" Lila whispered, obviously confused since we'd just been talking about Andy.

"Um, Lila," I whispered back, "not *now*."

"Oh, right, sorry," she said, giggling.

"Come on," I said, grabbing her arm and pulling her toward the door. "My cousin is always starting rumors. Let's just go—I have a free period next and I'm meeting Maria at the library. Come with?"

"Sure," Lila answered, shooting Veronica a dirty look in solidarity before leaving the classroom. "Now, let's forget about your cousin's attitude problem and get back to discussing the finer points of Andy Rotellini."

"Well, to be honest, he's one of my favorite topics," I said, laughing, feeling at the moment that Lila, as air-headed as she could be sometimes, might make a good Patron Saint of Loyalty.

9

I Drag Lila into the Dreary Library Stacks and Determine That I Need to Start Wearing a Bra on the Road to Sainthood

Hildegard, Hildegard, where are you?" I said under my breath, still half-listening to Lila, who'd followed me to the top of the old metal staircase that wove up the center of the library stacks like a fire escape, chatting the whole time about Chad Dawson, a sophomore hockey player from Bishop Francis. Holy Angels had quite a collection of saint biographies and other saint-related writings, though I was probably the only person who actually checked them out. I ran my fingers along the spines packed together tight on the shelf, crouching low, straining my eyes in the dim light. A cloud of dust hung in the air and I tried my best not to sneeze.

"I'm pretty sure he's not into Hilary because he spent most of yesterday before practice telling *me* about why Bishop Francis was going to win the season opener against LaSalle Prep."

"Hey, Lila, do you have a hair tie I could borrow?"

"Oh, sure," she said, digging into her purse and handing me a bright red band. "I really hope Hilary isn't into him, though, because that would be really uncool for us to like the same guy."

"You should just ask her," I said, doing my best to gather all my hair into a tight ponytail to prevent it from falling across my eyes.

"I'm worried she might actually say she *does* like him," Lila said, plopping down next to me. "And why are we way up here again?"

"You and I are here and not Maria because Maria has been here a gazillion times with me and she'd rather e-mail her boyfriend in the first-floor computer lab," I said, pulling the book I'd been searching for off the shelf, and releasing another cloud of dust into the air. My hands were gray with the filth of neglect. "And I wanted to find *this*." I held up the book so Lila could see the cover.

"Hildegard of Bingen, the *Scivias*," she read, mangling the pronunciation of *Scivias* as if it were "skeevi-as," as in skeevy old man.

"No, *Scivias* like 'civitas' but drop the *t*," I corrected her, feeling geeky for doing so. But then, spending all your free periods researching the saints *was* pretty geeky. It was important for me to know the history of the people whose ranks I was hoping to join—a crucial part of being a saint-in-training, since it wasn't like I could apply for saint school or anything. And anyhow, I loved their stories.

"Okay, so who is Hildegard and why do you care? Is this for a research paper or something?"

I wiped the remaining dust off the book with a tissue, and read out loud from the introduction. " 'Hildegard of Bingen was a visionary who acted as adviser to bishops, kings, and popes on matters of war, church laws, spiritual affairs, among other important issues, which is unusual for a woman of the twelfth century. The most powerful men of the day sought her counsel—including Frederick Barbarossa, the Holy Roman Emperor—believing that Hildegard had a special connection with God.' " Lila's eyes were beginning to glaze over but I plunged ahead anyway. "Hildegard was this amazing, bold woman, Lila, who didn't take no for an answer—not even from *the Pope*."

"That's cool," Lila said, distracted, taking out a mirror from her purse to apply lip gloss. "It's really a shame you're always putting your hair up, Antonia, because, seriously, you have the best hair out of anyone at HA. If I had your hair, I'd *always* wear it down."

Okay, so I couldn't expect everyone to be as enthralled with the saints as me.

But how could someone *not* see that Hildegard of Bingen was utterly exceptional? In addition to being a visionary (which means, well, Hildegard *saw* things, you know, visions of the Virgin Mary and Jesus and hell and some other really interesting stuff, which today may be grounds for being put in a mental institution but was normal for saints back in the day), Hildegard was a composer, an artist, a playwright, and a physician. Most remarkable, though, is the fact that Hildegard became famous throughout Europe *in her own time*. Meaning, *before* she died. Hildegard was practically a living saint—at least as close to one as I've ever encountered in my research. I took this as a sign of hope for my own aspirations—the bit about being alive to enjoy one's saintly status.

The only downer about Hildegard was her commitment to perpetual virginity. Hildegard was, you know, *a nun*. She was *really* devoted to this particular vow, too.

But, except for the visions, composing, artistic talent, and knowledge of all things herbal—areas in which I have no ability—we were practically twins! We both wrote letters to popes. We both gave them suggestions. And we both did this *before* death! I was obviously part of a Catholic girl feminist trend that stretched back for centuries.

There *was* the fact that we were both celibate to also consider—at least for the time being—but I pushed that thought from my mind as best as I could.

"Can we go back downstairs now?" Lila said, sneezing. "It's kind of creepy up here and my nose is starting to run."

"Yeah, I've got work to do before the bell rings anyway." We got up, brushing off our skirts, and began our spiral descent to the first floor, where we found Maria typing away at a computer in the corner.

"Did you get what you needed?" she asked when I sat down at the carrel next to hers.

"Yup," I said, dropping the heavy book so it made a loud thud on the desk.

"Did Lila have fun?"

"I'm not sure *fun* is the right word . . . it's more like she had allergies," I said, just as Lila let out another loud sneeze at a table nearby. Maybe I should propose a Patron Saint of Allergies next month.

"I tried to warn her," Maria said, shaking her head, and went back to her e-mailing.

Thinking about Hildegard made me wonder how I could beef up my saint résumé beyond my encyclopedic knowledge of all things saint-related and my history of letter writing to people in high church places. As an aspiring fifteen-year-old saint, what else should I be *doing*? How does a saint-to-be make her mark today? There was no way I was entering the convent, but if I was truly called to sainthood, then maybe I needed to be *doing* more saintly things on my way to great public renown.

I took out my Saint Diary and turned to the "Notes" section. After some thought, I began to write:

What Could Antonia Do? (WCAD?)
1. Stop giving my mother agita about my uniform (at least while I am still in the house) because even though some saints drove their mothers nuts during their lives (poor Monica, St. Augustine's mother, she just about didn't live through all her son's transgressions), I bet most of them had less, let's just say, <u>difficult</u> relationships with the women who bore them.
2. Instead of hoarding all chocolate to

myself and hiding it in my room and not offering it to others, even a piece, ever, because I regard all chocolate that comes into my possession as mine and not for the enjoyment of anyone else, I will be less selfish with my favorite sweet and give it away—most of it. Oooh! Perhaps especially to Andy since giving away chocolate might (a) give me a reason to speak to him and (b) make him notice me and think I was different from other girls, because, I mean, what teenage girl gives away chocolate of her own volition? Totally worth the sacrifice if it works.

3. Do more petitioning strictly on behalf of others and not just for myself because a good saint is always thinking of others, and some of them, like Julian of Norwich and Catherine of Siena, basically spent their whole lives in seclusion for the sole purpose of praying for other people. And, again, since I am not ever, in my right mind, entering a convent, perhaps doing a little more other-centered petitioning would be a saintlike thing I could do.

4. Wear a bra.

I admit, wearing a bra might not be the most obvious-sounding step toward sainthood, but here is the deal. Centuries ago—and still today among certain groups of the Catholic devout—saintly people believed that if they made their bodies as uncomfortable as possible to the point where they more or less tortured themselves, it would bring them closer to God. There were many preferred bodily discomforts to choose from, including—but not limited to—wearing a *hair shirt* (which is a tunic with scratchy, prickly things on the inside that hurt your skin), a cilice belt (which one might imagine as a spiky thigh garter that cuts into your leg when you walk—weirdly kinky and totally gross), self-flagellation (whipping yourself, and no, I am not kidding, people used to do this all the time), and, for the less masochistic, sleeping on a wooden board at night.

In my humble opinion, *wearing a bra every day* totally fit the virtual self-torture category given that (a) I absolutely didn't need one since I was a good deal flatter than the boards some of those people probably slept on and (b) was it just me, or did wearing a bra feel like you were strapped into some sort of a harness? Despite my mother's advice that girls my age should not go without one, I was pretty much antibra—not in a bra-burning way but more in a why-should-I-wear-something-totally-unnecessary-given-my-lack-of-boobs way. This made wearing a bra in the name of becoming more saintly a perfect idea because it was both uncomfortable and frugal since I already had a drawer full of them ready and waiting at home.

I would start wearing a bra *tomorrow*.

I felt more saintly already.

We still had twenty minutes before the end-of-school bell, so I decided to do some virtual-Vatican-fig-tree-follow-up before I actually had to deal with the real fig trees tomorrow. I logged onto my e-mail account and began typing.

To: askthevatican@vatican.va

From: Antonia Lucia Labella [STMP: saint2b@live.com]

Subject: Patron Saint of Figs request

Sent: November 18, 2:43 p.m.

Attachment: *antoniaschoolpic.jpg*

To Whom It May Concern (ideally the Pope if he's available):

This is just a follow-up to my letter from earlier this month about the dire need among Catholics worldwide for a Patron Saint of Figs. This saint would be important not only for fig-eaters (fig-eaters are a devoted sort of people which is already a good sign for needing a saint, i.e., people who eat figs *really* love them) but also for fig tree caretakers everywhere. I am about to spend an entire 48 hours of my life winterizing the fig trees in the backyard of our family store (I may have said something about that in my letter) and having a saint specialty for figs would be really helpful in getting through this process. Since there is already a Patron Saint for RUNNING WATER, I don't think it's too much to ask to add someone who specializes in figs to the list.

Again, I am available for the job if you need someone. I'm attaching my latest school picture so you can update my file.

Thanks for your time!

Blessings,
Antonia Lucia Labella
Labella's Market of Federal Hill
33 Atwells Avenue
Providence, RI USA
saint2b@live.com

P.S. You should know that I am kind of a minor miracle magnet lately. By minor I mean, you know, little stuff like avoiding familial conflict by praying for my cousin to stay away from work and then finding out my prayer was answered and she was home sick with the flu, thus saving my mother hours of grief.

Wait. Maybe Francesca's coming down with the flu and staying home from the market was not the most becoming of miracles to which I could attach myself in an effort to win over the Vatican and change saint history. I backspaced. Little stuff like *what*?

little stuff like the love of my life actually showing up during my shift at work

No. Revealing my adolescent sexual interests to the
Vatican was probably not the best idea either.

little stuff like my playing like a virtual varsity soccer star
in gym the other day.

No. That was insignificant to the point of too negli-
gible to mention. There really *was* a pretty long list of
minor miraculous events this week though—even Billy
Bruno's same-day elbow healing, which was far more
appropriate to mention than Francesca's flu symptoms
and my newfound soccer abilities. I decided to go for
broke:

P.S. You should know that I am kind of a minor miracle
magnet lately. By minor I mean, you know, little things like
my elderly neighbor, Mrs. Bevalaqua, who has had serious arthritis and all sorts of leg problems that were so
bad she was in a wheelchair for twenty years, and, *just
like that*, a few petitions to St. Sebastian and the woman
is walking again! Totally extraordinary. Not that I really
think I had a hand in this wondrous occurrence, it's just
that I thought you should know in case you were interested. Hope to see you soon and look forward to hearing
what you think of the new picture!

Just as I clicked Send, the bell rang. Maria, Lila, and I jumped up, grabbing our things. Lila waved goodbye and went running off to meet Hilary and Angela and their Bishop Francis hockey boys, and Maria waited while I checked out my Hildegard book so we could enjoy my one free afternoon of the week.

"This is due back December first," Mrs. Gaines, the school librarian, said as she scanned my book into the computer.

December first, I thought. That was soon. Would I be proposing a new saint that day or finally basking in the glow of beatification? Had I gone overboard adding that "minor miracle magnet" bit in the e-mail? No, I decided. There couldn't be enough miracle talk for an aspiring saint. Miracles were just a part of my everyday existence, so *of course* it was important—imperative even—to mention them to The Vatican People. I had to put my best foot forward, right? I had nothing to lose after all.

Well, except my life. But what was a little death when the community of saints awaited?

10

MARIA AND I GOSSIP AT THE ICE RINK,
AND SHE HANDS MY INNOCENCE TO MICHAEL IN
EXCHANGE FOR SOME ALONE-TIME WITH JOHN

*L*ila overheard you say *what* in Sister Mary Margaret's class?"

"My passionate petition to St. Jude that I, Antonia Lucia Labella, was desperate to kiss Andy Rotellini, come hell, high water, and even death," I said. "Well, I didn't really *say* anything about hell, high water, or death to Jude, but you get the picture."

"And then Veronica made a scene?"

"Yup."

Maria and I were skating in slow circles around her family's ice rink during the free skate she worked two days a week after school. We were still wearing our uniform plaid. Maria's pretty dark hair flowed behind her as we moved, making me wish mine was straight, too. It was so cold in the arena I could see my breath. I puffed into my red-mittened hands, feeling the warmth against my face. Little kids wobbled along the ice with their parents nearby, and middle school aspiring hockey players—both girls and boys—sped past Maria and me as if we were standing still.

"Seriously. What is Veronica's problem with you? With everybody, for that matter?"

"Well, you already know the family history," I said. "And then Veronica doesn't know how to have more than one friend at a time, so when you showed up, three became a crowd."

"Antonia," I heard a little-girl voice calling suddenly. I turned and saw Bennie (short for Bennedicta), Maria's baby sister, skating up. She wrapped her arms around my legs, almost knocking me over. "Antonia," she yelled again.

When I'd recovered my balance, I bent down to give her a hug. She squeezed me as hard as a five-year-old's arms could manage. "What did you do in kindergarten today?"

"Well, I painted this picture of my family and it had Mom and Dad and Maria and James and Adriana and Pia and . . ."

"Hey, squirt, that's enough," Maria said, interrupting Bennie, which allowed Bennie to finally take in a much-needed breath. Unlike me, Maria came from a huge family—she was the oldest.

"But—"

"Remember what Mom said about interrupting people? Antonia and I were having a conversation."

"I was just saying hi," she said, starting to pout. "To Antonia, *not you*," she spat with such force that she went sprawling forward onto the ice.

"Oh, Bennie," Maria sighed, skating over to help her up.

"Go away," Bennie said, her face scrunched up, obviously trying not to cry. "I want Antonia," she whined.

"Hey, fine, whatever you want, kiddo." Maria backed away, her hands in the air. To me she said with a nod, "Go ahead, St. Antonia, my baby sister needs you."

"I'm not a baby." Bennie's eyes welled with tears.

"Let me see, Bennie," I said, and Bennie held up both of her hands. They were scraped raw from skidding against the ice. "I think you need to go see your dad at the first-aid station, but," I said, taking both hands gently, "I think you need a couple of kisses to start the healing process, right, Maria?"

"Whatever you say, St. Antonia," she agreed.

"Okay," Bennie said, watching as I lightly kissed each palm. "They already feel better now." She smiled and skated off in a flash, her pink corduroyed legs moving like lightning toward the exit door, her scrapes quickly forgotten.

"Before that little interruption," Maria said as we began moving again, "I was about to tell you not to blame me for Veronica's problems."

"I wasn't blaming you, I was just implying that Veronica was a jealous girl . . ."

"Whatever," she said. "New topic: So you basically told Lila how you feel about Andy Rotellini?"

"Yup. And she was totally cool about it. I don't know why I worry so much about other people knowing who I like or . . ." I stopped, midsentence.

"The fact that you secretly aspire to be the first living saint in Catholic history?"

"Maybe."

"It is a little unusual!"

"Don't tell me you aren't looking forward to the day when you become Maria Romano, best friend in the whole world to Antonia, Patron Saint of Something or Other."

"Calm down," Maria said, zipping up her "Romano Arena" jacket and adjusting her blue scarf so it was tight around her neck. Maria's skirt was hiked so short you could tell she was not even wearing boxers underneath. Her legs were red from the cold. "You can be confident that I will always be supportive of all your clandestine endeavors."

"Not always. But almost always," I called out as Maria skated off to deal with two little boys who looked like they were about to come to blows.

A little more than a year ago I suggested a Patron Saint of Irons and Ironing, which Maria judged as temporary insanity on my part. Gram had almost burned the whole house down, market and all, by forgetting to unplug the iron, so it seemed like a good idea at the time. But Maria was horrified by the possibility that this might be the idea that would finally get through to the Vatican, and then she would be known as The Best Friend of the new Patron Saint of Irons and Ironing.

"Do you really want pictures of yourself in some dowdy housedress holding an iron in your hand all over the place, Antonia?" Maria said at the time. "I can see it now—*Still Life: Girl with Iron* in every Catholic church for miles around."

She'd had a point. Not much glamorous portrait potential in ironing.

The saints each had their own representations—you know, a particular way they were always pictured related to their talent. Like Sebastian's sexy, muscular bod since he represented athletes.

And figs! Figs were a sexy sort of fruit. Figs had lots of potential for the saint portrait. I could be holding a fig to my lips, for example. With a lusty look in my eyes . . . Or I could be reaching for a fig in a tree. My chin tilted toward heaven, my black hair cascading wildly down my back. A little sliver of midriff showing. Yes. This was good.

Sometimes Maria tried to help me with saint suggestions, but she always came up with ideas that would never work.

Like breast augmentation. Or instant slimness. Not that she needed to worry about those things.

The Vatican People would never go for that anyway.

Things to Remember When Suggesting Saint Specializations
- Can't majorly conflict with nature (i.e., the way God made things)
- Has to help make the world a better place, even if in a small way (e.g., providing consolation for

sadness, feeding the poor, keeping the breast milk flowing. Yes, there is actually a saint for breast-feeding)

- Specializations that help with everyday activities = good
- Anything to do with Sex, especially kinky-happy-sexy pleasure = bad

Making boobs bigger and reducing the circumference of thighs fails all four.

"Little boys are monsters," Maria said once she'd caught up to where I was still moving along, talking over the *click-click* of everyone's skates against the ice.

"Is John coming by today?"

"Not until after soccer practice," Maria answered. She took my arms and we did a little spin so she was skating backward.

"I thought soccer season was over."

"Well, it *is* over, but apparently they practice indoors during the winter."

"So I'm stuck being your only rink buddy?" No sooner was this out of my mouth than a familiar Irish brogue called out from behind me.

"Hello, loves!"

"Um, Antonia, there's something I've been meaning to mention," Maria whispered, grabbing my arms.

"That Michael is now working Friday afternoons?" I hissed.

"Am I interrupting something?" Michael said, sliding to a stop beside us, sending up a wave of ice from the force. He wore a black jacket and hockey skates like Maria.

"Aren't you a little late today for your shift?"

"Who are you, my boss now?" Michael asked Maria, skating backward with ease. If I hadn't known better I'd have thought he was a hockey player. Michael was athletic even if he didn't play any sports. We were moving faster now and the cold air raised goose bumps on my legs, and for once I wished I was wearing tights.

"Um, yeah, I sort of am your boss," Maria answered. "Don't worry, though. I won't tell my dad."

"Kind *and* beautiful. What a combination," Michael said, his tone sarcastic. "You're awfully quiet, Antonia. Though I couldn't help but notice you had plenty to say to Maria before I showed up. Don't let me stop you from your conversation." He slowed a bit and skated closer, his stare unnerving as usual.

"Well, you interrupted a private discussion," I answered, giving him my best don't-mess-with-me stare when a pint-sized hockey-player-in-training whizzed by. He knocked me off balance and sent me sprawling. I could hear Maria laughing and trying not to laugh all at once.

"Damsel in distress on the ice," Michael said with mischief. "I'll handle this one, Maria."

"Go right ahead." Maria said as she watched me trying to pull down my uniform skirt, which had flown up virtually around my neck when I fell. Thank God *somebody* wore boxers today, otherwise I would have flashed half the neighborhood, young and old, not to mention Michael McGinnis.

Michael leaned over, his right hand stretched out to me. "Need some help, love?"

"Sure, I guess, since no one else is offering," I said, shooting Maria an accusing look. I took Michael's hand and felt myself pulled up from the ice, my skirt falling back into place. Michael grabbed my waist to steady me, but didn't show signs of letting go even after I'd regained my balance.

"Thanks," I said, trying to take my hand back, but his grip was firm. His eyes were intense, staring into mine, and I found I couldn't move. His hand felt warm against my body. My heart thudded in my chest. "What are you doing?" I finally asked, trying to recover my senses. "Can I have my hand back, please?"

"Your cheeks are as red as your mittens."

"It's the cold, don't flatter yourself," I lied, wiggling out of his grip and skating over to Maria.

"If you want me to leave you two alone, no worries," Maria said loud enough for Michael to hear.

"Some best friend you are today," I said, hooking my arm back into hers, pushing off my left toe pick. "You know I don't like to be left alone with him."

"Why is it that I scare you so much, Antonia? You should really give that some thought . . ." Michael called out from behind us.

"You don't scare me," I yelled back. "I am *not* intimidated by my friends." Whether I was trying to convince myself, Michael, Maria, or all three of us of this was unclear.

"So we're *just* friends, eh?" His voice had mock hurt in it.

"*Just* friends."

"And stop checking out our legs, Michael," Maria chimed in.

"I will if you let me in on the conversation."

"Okay, keep checking them out, then."

"Maria! Stop encouraging him," I protested.

"How 'bout you let me give Antonia a ride home later and I won't bother you anymore for the rest of the free skate."

"Deal, Michael," Maria said.

"Maria! You want me to get in his *car*?" My mouth dropped open in surprise at Maria's willingness to sacrifice my safety in exchange for peace and quiet now.

"I just did us a favor," she said, her face all innocence. "He'll leave us alone now, which is what you wanted anyway. *Right?*"

"I guess," I answered, feeling unsure about what I really did and didn't want when it came to Michael McGinnis.

"Besides, I can't take you home later because John is supposed to meet me here when soccer gets out."

"But what if Michael tries something, Maria?" I shivered thinking about it.

"Then maybe you can practice on him," she said, giving me a playful jab. This was not the answer I expected. "Antonia, if he *did* try something again, maybe it wouldn't be a bad thing. Maybe it would force you guys to figure out whatever is going on between the two of you."

"We *so* have nothing going on, you know that. And there's no way I'm kissing Michael, practice or no," I assured Maria.

"I remember a time when you actually *wanted* to kiss Michael. Dreamed about it. Almost as much as you do now with Andy," she whispered.

"That was a long time ago, when I was young and foolish and didn't know what I was getting into with him."

"And you do now?"

"Well, no. I don't know. Not exactly, I guess," I said, picking at the ice with my skate. "Okay, I'll admit that sometimes I am not so sure what's between us—if there's anything still between us. Which is also why I avoid all Michael-Antonia-alone-time, as you already know, Maria."

"Nothing is going to happen, Antonia. It's just a ride home."

"You saw how he's acting."

"He's just playing around. You said it yourself—you guys are just friends."

"I hope he agrees with you on that one."

"Well, I think you have nothing to worry about."

"That's not what you said the other day in the parking lot," I said, remembering the conversation. "Besides, you just didn't want to get stuck driving me home when you could be alone with John." I was starting to panic. "Maria, Michael is *notorious*."

"Listen," Maria said, yanking me into a corner of the rink, her hands firm on my shoulders, holding me steady. "I am confident that Michael would *never* do anything to hurt you or pull any of that crap he pulls on the other girls who fall for him. He respects you too much. Anyone with eyes and ears can figure that out."

"I just get so nervous around him."

"You may be worrying over nothing after all. *Apparently*, he already has his next conquest in sight, if Veronica is to be believed," Maria said, glancing behind her to make sure Michael wasn't nearby.

"Veronica? Are you crazy? No way would Michael *ever* go for her." I was so taken aback I almost fell again. Maria grabbed my arm, steadying me. "Though that might explain why she's gone from merely nasty to intolerably awful lately."

"Well, during free period this morning I was studying in the cafeteria when I heard Veronica, a few tables away, telling Concetta how she is totally into Michael and she's convinced he has feelings for her. Though nothing has happened yet."

"She said that loud enough so you could hear?"

"Oh, yeah. I think she wanted me to because she knew I'd report this information to you."

"Veronica and Michael?" I felt nauseous. The thought of my cousin and Michael together was . . . was . . . inconceivable . . . I just couldn't imagine it . . . but it wasn't just that . . . it just didn't sit right. I couldn't understand why I felt so upset. It was *Michael*, not Andy. If it had been Andy she'd been blathering on about, then it would make sense that I'd be angry. And Michael had no allegiance to me and, well, if he could make Veronica happy somehow, then who was I to stand in their way? It would probably be better for all of us if Veronica was in a better mood. Right?

"Are you okay? You look a little green . . ."

"I'm fine," I lied.

". . . because that's not all she said," Maria went on. "Veronica also mentioned that she thinks Michael is even better looking than *Andy*."

"Veronica compared Michael to Andy?" I asked, beginning to wonder if Veronica had somehow found out I liked him. "Why does she have to get in the way of my love life in addition to everything else?"

"Everybody thinks Andy's hot, you know that. It may have just been a coincidence."

"I hate Veronica," I said, my voice faint.

"Antonia, *breathe*. Let's switch topics to something less upsetting to you . . . like your quest for sainthood and how the Vatican is totally going to name you the Patron Saint of Figs and Fig Trees any day now," Maria said, giving my arm a squeeze.

"Okay. Good idea," I agreed, squeezing back, trying to compose myself, unclear why I was so upset. Maria and I continued circling the rink, each lap moving us closer to the time when the Zamboni would come out to clear the ice and Michael would chauffeur me home.

11

MICHAEL DRIVES ME HOME AND WE
SHARE A MOMENT

·

I'll get that," Michael said, opening the passenger door.

It was five p.m. and already dark. The almost wintry cold was making me shiver. I prayed:

Come on, St. Sebaldus, O Patron Saint Against Cold Weather, can't you help with the temperature? The last thing I need is Michael trying to warm me up.

"Aren't you the gentleman today?" I said out loud to Michael as I slipped into the seat, while he stood there, still holding the door. Not only was Michael opening doors but he had offered to carry my backpack. He practically had to rip it out of my arms on our way out of the rink, but still, he managed.

"I know how to treat the ladies."

"I notice you said 'ladies' in the plural."

"I am a gentleman to *all* the girls."

"So I've heard," I said, grabbing my backpack from him. "From just about everyone in my class. And the class above mine. And even some of the seniors."

"All lies . . ." Michael said while shutting the door, his eyes sparkling with mischief.

I took a deep breath, trying to calm myself down as Michael walked around the front of the car. Something was on the seat and I pulled it out from under my legs. It was *The Providence Journal*. I smiled when I read the headline: MIRACLE ON ATWELLS AVE.! LOCAL WOMAN WALKS FOR FIRST TIME IN 20 YEARS

In the photograph Mrs. Bevalaqua looked pretty—she was dressed in a ladylike suit, with full makeup and gloves of course, her gray hair pulled up and away from her face. My nervousness about Michael melted away as I skimmed through the article. Mrs. B mentioned me several times. Interesting.

"Girls at your school love to gossip about hooking up with Bishop Francis guys," Michael said as he got in the driver's seat.

"Funny how the one they all pick to gossip about is *you*."

"You're wrong about me, Antonia," Michael countered as he put the car in reverse, but instead of backing out he gave me a long look and then put the car back into park. "Why are you so happy suddenly? Is it something you realized about me? Like maybe the fact that you secretly love all the attention I give you?" His eyes flashed. They looked a deep blue in the darkness. He grinned as he leaned in my direction, waiting for my response.

"You *wish*, Michael. You are *so forward* sometimes," I answered, feeling that familiar nervousness come over me again. I smoothed my skirt so it almost reached my knees. "And I'm smiling because I just saw the story about Mrs. Bevalaqua in the paper." I shoved the newspaper between us like a shield, so he could see the article.

"It's incredible," Michael answered. His voice held a genuineness I wasn't used to. "They even got the headline right."

"What do you mean?"

"The part about the miracle."

"You think so?"

"I do," he said with confidence. For once I didn't want to turn away, so we sat there, eyes locked, my brown pouring into his blue and vice versa.

"Do you *really* think it was a miracle, what happened to Mrs. Bevalaqua?"

"Yeah, I do, Antonia," he said.

"Really? *Really* really? Do you believe in them, then? You know, miracles?"

"Well, look at her," Michael said, grabbing the paper and holding it between us. "She's walking after twenty years."

"Yeah, I know," I said, sighing.

"What about *you*? Do you believe in miracles?" He threw the paper into the backseat and turned to face me again. His hand lingered at the edge of my seat, not even an inch away from my skirt.

A long moment of silence hung between us. I tried to ignore the thrill I felt with him so close. "I think miracles happen all the time," I began, then paused. "And some are bigger or, I guess, more *noticeable* than others." Somewhere in the back of my mind it registered that Michael and I were beginning to have a real conversation, the kind we always had that first summer when we met. This unexpected intimacy made me bold. "I think it's the saints, you know. I think they are around us all the time, in our lives, listening to our prayers. Making miracles."

"Do you think of your father as a saint?" he asked out of the blue, catching me off guard, as if he were somehow inside my mind, poking around, looking through a file of my deepest secrets, or reading my soul. Michael and I had never once spoken about my father. The look in his eyes was serious, gentle even.

"Not exactly, no," I began my answer, thinking about how I loved Michael's question, that he'd even wonder whether I thought of my dad as a saint. "My dad loved the saints, though. He was named after one actually. As was yours truly," I added.

"He was? You were? Which one? I mean, I don't know your father's name, I guess. And there's a St. Antonia then, I assume . . ."

"I'll tell you about my dad first," I said, pressing at the creases in my skirt, my hand brushing Michael's for one, electric second. "His name was Genesioso," I explained, pronouncing each vowel carefully, drawing out the long *e* and *o* sounds. "Most people called him Gino for short."

"And he died when you were little, right?" Michael shifted position so he was almost facing me, moving his hand to the passenger-side headrest, his fingers so close to the back of my neck I could feel their warmth. He seemed willing for us to sit there idling in the parking lot all night.

"I had just turned seven when he died."

"What do you remember about him?"

"Well, he had the perfect saint name for his personality," I said, smiling, the words coming easier now. "St. Genesius is the Patron Saint of Actors, Drama, Comedians, Clowns, and Dancers, and my dad was quite the clown. A fantastic dancer, too. He and my mother went out dancing a lot when I was little. Gram would stay home to babysit me. They used to have a good time, I think — my mom and dad. My mother hasn't danced once since he died. They were beautiful to watch . . ."

"She must miss him a lot."

"Yeah . . . we all do. It's hard," I said, looking away. I was afraid I might cry.

Michael changed the subject, as if he could sense that I needed to talk about something else. I turned to face him again and saw that familiar look of mischief return to his eyes. I felt a rush of gratitude.

"Technically I was named after St. Anthony, the Finder

of Lost Things," I began, but Michael chimed in at "Anthony" and finished the sentence without me.

"I sense a 'but' in that statement, Antonia."

"Well, you will just have to look up St. Antonia yourself because I'm *not* telling you that one. It's way too embarrassing."

"You know a lot about saints, don't you?"

"Yes. I suppose so. Don't all Catholics?"

"Well, when most Catholics are asked to describe their father, most would *not* compare him to his name saint."

"Oh. Maybe not."

"And back when you and I used to"—he paused a moment, searching for words to describe "us" and our past activities—"*hang out*, you'd always bring up some saint or other in conversation."

"So?"

"So nobody I know does that. Not even my grandmother."

"I read a lot."

"What's the fascination?"

"I'll tell you . . . if you tell me . . . whether or not one of my cousins is next on your list of conquests?" The question was out of my mouth before I could catch it.

"Why do you care so much about me and other girls? What is it that bugs you, Antonia?"

"You're not answering my question."

"You're not answering mine."

"You first," I said, unwilling to budge. Besides, I didn't know the answer to his question. I wished I did.

"I think you may have inherited your father's dramatic traits." Michael's eyebrows arched.

"My mother is the drama queen in the family — *not* me," I said in my defense.

"But what I am really wondering now is whether you inherited your father's ability for dancing . . ."

"Why would you care about *that*?" I said, getting nervous. Was he asking because of the HA–Bishop Francis Winter Formal coming up? *Was he going to ask me to go with him?* Maybe I was getting ahead of myself and Michael was just making conversation. Oh, why was talking to a boy so fraught with complication?

"Just curious, that's all," he answered quickly, sensing my discomfort.

"Okay," I said, unsure what else to add. The intimacy between us was suddenly gone, bursting like a fragile bubble. And I felt . . . disappointed. Even though, I reminded myself, Andy was the love of my life and the boy I'd been waiting to kiss for fifteen years. I wasn't about to settle for anyone else. Not that kissing Michael would be settling since I was sure he was a perfectly good kisser — it's just that I wasn't going to find that out, myself.

Michael sighed, shifting positions again so that he could finally back out of the parking space. We left the lot and drove in silence, passing fast-food restaurants and strip malls until we neared Federal Hill, where things started to look more like a neighborhood again. I stared out the passenger window, noticing that some of the houses already had decorations outside for Christmas. It wasn't even Thanksgiving yet. I did my best to pay attention to everything *but* the tension that ebbed and flowed between Michael and me.

"Are you giving me the silent treatment?" Michael spoke for the first time since we left the skating rink.

"No, I've been praying to St. John about our friendship," I said without thinking, even though I hadn't been.

"See. You *are* always going on about the saints, Antonia."

"I had saints on my mind because we were just talking about them—that's all." I turned to Michael and added, "St. John is the Patron Saint of Friends and Friendship."

"I know who St. John is," Michael said. "What about?"

"What about what?"

"The prayer to St. John. What was it about?"

"Oh. That we don't let any weirdness get in the way of us being friends again," I said, making up an answer on the spot. But as soon as I'd said it, I knew that I meant it. I'd been enjoying our talk—it reminded me of how I felt when Michael and I first met, like we could talk for hours.

"What do you mean, *weirdness*?"

"I don't know, Michael," I said, sighing. And I really didn't. "Can you let me out here, please?"

"We're still a block from your house."

"Yes, but I'm only allowed to ride in Maria's car." I dug in my backpack for my keys. "If my mother, or anyone in the family, for that matter, sees me getting out of your car, I'll be in trouble."

"But it's Friday, Antonia, I thought we could—"

"NO. I can't," I said before he could finish.

"Whatever, Antonia," Michael said. There was frustration in his voice. He pulled the car over.

"Whatever, Michael," I said, getting out of the car. I slammed the door and stomped off without looking back, my brain turning a mile a minute. How could I go from a place where I felt totally connected to Michael, like I could trust him in this really important way, back to tense and confusing in, like, zero seconds? And besides, our relationship—or whatever you wanted to call it—wasn't always about me. It was usually about *him* and what he wanted to know or what he wanted me to do. Though there was one thing I felt sure about: my personality didn't vanish into thin air around Michael like it did when I was around other boys, like, say, well, *Andy*, for example. But then, that was just because I didn't know Andy as well.

I stopped walking as a wave of guilt hit me. I hadn't even thanked Michael for the ride. I turned around to run back to the car and make amends, but I was already too late.

I watched as Michael's car peeled away, leaving me alone, confused, my heart pounding so hard I wondered if anyone passing on the sidewalk could hear it.

12

I Worry About My Fig Proposal, and "The Anti-Angel" Pays Me a Visit

It was late and my awkward goodbye with Michael already felt like it had happened a long time ago. I had other things to worry about at the moment. *Big* things. Literally.

My Saint Diary lay open to St. Charles Borromeo. The soft glow of my reading lamp illumined the good archbishop, also the Patron Saint of Apple Orchards. I was considering whether to petition him for the fig-tree burying this weekend. He was a poor substitute for what I really needed, though.

An apple tree is *nothing* like a fig tree.

Which is why we needed a Patron Saint of Figs and Fig Trees. Though I admit I was starting to lose hope. November was passing quickly and my calendar reminded me that it was already that time of the month, the time I began brainstorming other possible saint proposals in case the current campaign was unsuccessful. By the first of December I would have my next letter drafted and ready to go.

I needed to be prepared.

It was eighteen uneventful days into the Month of Figs, and the list of things that *hadn't* happened during the current campaign for sainthood were many:

News from the Vatican that they loved my Patron Saint of Figs idea: Nope.

News from the Vatican that they not only loved my Patron Saint of Figs idea but had elected me as their ideal candidate for the job: Not so far, no.

Getting my mother to let me off the hook about winterizing the fig trees: Not happening.

Finding out that the love of my life knew I existed: Not that I knew of.

Success in the Kissing-the-Love-of-My-Life department: Not this week.

My capacity for patience growing: Nope again.

My brain stalled. Usually I was full of new saint ideas, but tonight I was empty. I turned to the section in my Saint Diary where I kept a record of the year's proposals, hoping for inspiration. Last month, October, was the Month of Secrets and Secret Keeping. I couldn't believe the Catholic Church didn't have a Patron Saint of Secrets, someone devoted to not gossiping, spreading rumors, and sharing people's deepest desires. September was the Month of Memory, which I'd proposed with Gram in mind.

I knew I could use a Patron Saint of Memory where Gram was concerned. But, for now, at least I had St. Anne. I picked up my pen and began to write:

Dear St. Anne, O Patron Saint of Grandmothers, please watch over Editta Lucia Goglia, who I love so much it almost hurts, because I am worried about her and this whole forgetting and misplacing everything but the kitchen sink business. I don't know what I'd do without her, so if you could please send some attention her way I'd be forever grateful. Thank you, St. Anne, for your intercession in this matter.

The St. Anne mass card in my Saint Diary was one of my favorites—a woman sat, serene, a halo glowing above her. One arm was raised up toward heaven and the other was around a child, a little girl kneeling next to her. The girl's eyes gazed lovingly up at this gentle lady. I stuffed the petition in the pocket on St. Anne's page.

I rolled onto my back and closed my eyes, feeling tired. I needed a good night's sleep for the big day tomorrow. Inspiration was unlikely at this hour, so I forced myself to get up and put my Saint Diary away and then slipped back into bed. I tucked the blankets all around my body until I was cozy and warm, ready to let go of the day into sleep.

As I was drifting off I fantasized about Andy's first day

at the market (which was tomorrow!) . . . we'd accidentally gotten locked in the storeroom overnight . . . the lights
were out and we were *all alone* . . . I was pressed against
a wall of boxes and Andy was leaning toward me, about
to kiss me for the first time . . . when right at that very moment . . .

. . . there was an urgent *tap, tap, tap* against my window.
I sat up with a jolt.

I couldn't even get kissed by a boy in my dreams.

I dragged myself out of bed and wrapped myself up in
my rose-colored quilt. I turned on the light and opened the
window.

"What are you doing here?"

"I just thought I'd say hello again, love." Michael
McGinnis was crouched outside on the landing as if it
were totally normal to be sitting there like a burglar.

"By climbing up the fire escape at midnight?" It had
been more than a year since Michael had last come to my
window. He used to do it all the time until my mother almost caught him—well, *us*—which would have gotten me
grounded for the rest of my natural-born life. "My mother
would kill you if she found you here. And *me*. She'd kill
me."

"Your mother loves me," he said with confidence.

"My mother only loves boys who show no interest in
her daughter."

"So you think I'm showing interest?"

"I didn't mean *that*," I said, getting flustered, especially
since it was hard to ignore that Michael looked good. He

wore a thick winter jacket with a blue wool scarf that matched the color of his eyes.

"What *did* you mean?" He leaned forward far enough that his head almost came inside the room.

"I don't know what I meant. Can we change the subject? Like to why you didn't see enough of me earlier?" Maybe Michael wasn't mad at me after all.

"Well, no one should be alone on a Friday night. How about you let me climb in so we can chat awhile?" He glanced around my bedroom with interest.

"Not unless you want to get me in trouble," I said, though I did pull my vanity chair over to the window. "Besides, I'm not letting you anywhere near my bed."

"I learned my lesson about you a long time ago, Antonia . . ."

"What's that supposed to mean?"

"We're just friends, like you said, so you have nothing to worry about. I'm happy to simply talk through the window even if I am a bit chilled." He rubbed his hands together.

"Well, aren't you nice," I said, getting up to grab my red mittens off the vanity and handing them to him out the window. "I think these are big enough."

"Thanks," he said, putting them on.

"I like your pajamas. The bottoms are a bit big for you, though," he said, reminding me that when I'd gone to get the mittens I'd left the quilt behind. I was now sitting there, in only the thin white tank top I'd worn to bed and my billowy striped pajama pants. I quickly rolled myself back up in the quilt.

"Don't feel like you have to hide anything from me, Antonia." Michael's voice was teasing, his face only inches from mine through the window.

"Yeah, right," I said, pulling the blanket tighter.

"I don't just mean your pajamas, Antonia. You don't have to hide other things either . . ." He trailed off.

"Like what other things?"

"Like . . . well . . . for example . . . who do you have your eye on these days? You know, who do you like?"

"Seriously? We can't talk about that kind of stuff. That's girl talk."

"It's *friend* talk," he countered.

"Well, yes, that's true."

"Which is exactly why I was asking. If we are friends we should be able to talk about anything."

"You really want to know?" I'd trusted Lila about Andy and that went well—but Michael? Then again, maybe talking to him about who I liked would finally shift our relationship from this weird, awkward stage to a place where we could actually hang out like normal people. Like, *friends*. I mean, if I was honest, I missed Michael and how things used to be between us. *A lot.*

"I am burning with curiosity about it actually." His eyes were playful, but behind them lurked something else. I couldn't decide what.

"There *is* someone," I began, dangling the beginnings

of a confession, not certain how far I'd go yet. "He's actually in your class. But I am not going to tell you who it is."

"Come on. You can trust me. Scout's honor."

"Like you were ever a Boy Scout," I snickered.

"Okay . . . if you won't tell me who he is"—Michael paused, thinking—"then will you at least tell me whether or not you and he are already . . . *involved* in some way?" His tone was lighthearted, but there was an urgency in it too, and I wondered if there was another reason Michael was outside my window—one that he wasn't telling me.

"No, we are not at this moment *involved*. I'm not involved with anyone," I admitted.

"So you like someone but you're not going out with him?" He sounded relieved.

"The boy hardly even knows I exist and I can't go out with someone who doesn't know I exist."

"*I* know you exist."

This comment didn't even justify a response so instead I just rolled my eyes.

"I *do*, though," he insisted.

"I know you do . . . like a brother, Michael," I said, deciding to play his game a bit since he was always turning our conversations into DTR's: determining the relationship talks. "You're like an older brother who's looking out for his little sister and her love interests."

"Ouch. That's just about the worst thing you could ever say to a guy."

"What is?"

"Rule number one: Never tell a guy he's like a brother unless he actually *is* your brother. You may as well stab him in the heart."

"I was kidding. Calm down."

"Yeah, well, regardless of whether or not we're being all *friendly*, I don't want to hear any more talk about me being your brother, please," he said, shifting so his knees came up beneath his chin. "Is that how you *really* think about me?"

I thought about the ambiguity in our relationship and decided to be honest. "No. I've never thought of you that way. I said it so you'd stop pestering me. Seriously. You're not exactly the brotherly type, Michael."

"Well, that's good to hear. I think. But can you elaborate on what you mean by I'm not the brotherly type?" There he was, trying to turn the conversation back to "us" again.

"You're too . . . I don't know . . . you're so flirty, like, all the time. And with *everybody*." I couldn't help taking the bait. "And there's the fact that you've kissed just about every girl at my school."

"You exaggerate."

"I don't think so."

"I haven't kissed *you*, Antonia," Michael said without skipping a beat, and we were suddenly outside of friend-to-friend territory again.

"No, you haven't," I said with a nervous laugh. "Because we're just friends, remember?"

"We weren't always."

"Well, but technically we never got together that summer."

"It's not like I didn't try." His eyes locked on mine.

"I know," I said, looking away, thinking about how this was the first time Michael and I had ever openly acknowledged what happened—or, really, *didn't* happen—between us that day when he tried to kiss me and I ran away. I'd been winding my way through the labyrinth of bathhouses where people kept their beach chairs and umbrellas, looking for the ladies' room. Michael worked nearby and I knew I'd run into him. I mean, I'd wanted to see him. I *always* did, even though seeing him gave me that jittery feeling inside.

Michael was the first boy, really the *only* boy, who'd ever paid attention to me in the way that boys who like girls pay attention.

I just wasn't prepared for him to try to kiss me.

I turned a corner, heading down the row that led to the bathroom, when I saw him, leaning against the salt-worn wood of one of the bathhouse doors, its white paint peeling everywhere.

"Hey, Antonia," he said casually. "I was hoping I'd see you today."

My heart skipped, seeing him here, as if he'd been waiting for me.

"I need to talk to you," he said, walking up until he was so close I fought the urge to take a step back.

"About what?" I forced myself to look straight into his eyes, trying to read what they were saying. I shifted nervously from my left leg to my right.

"About what's going to happen when school starts."

"What do you mean?"

"Between you and me," he answered, tilting his head.

"We'll still be friends," I said, now staring at my feet, afraid of what might happen.

He put his hands on my shoulders, making me shiver. I worried that my legs would no longer support my body. "Look at me," he said. "Please?"

So I did.

"I like you, Antonia," he said simply, and my heart felt as if it had just dropped through my body and crashed through the boardwalk onto the sand beneath. "A lot," he added.

My hands began shaking. My whole body began shaking. I didn't know what to do or say so I said nothing.

"What are you thinking?"

"That I feel the same," I whispered, not able to say the words "I like you" out loud, scared out of my mind, totally unprepared for what came next, which was Michael leaning toward me, his blue-green eyes still locked on mine, his mouth parted and . . .

. . . at that moment the entire summer flashed before me—all those times Michael and I spent hanging out, all the girls he'd been with, all the intensity between us, the wanting but not wanting, the confusion—and I knew right then *that I wasn't ready*. He was out of my league. Way too experienced. It just couldn't happen between Michael and me. Not at that moment. Maybe not ever.

Then I panicked.

And before his lips could meet mine I turned and ran, leaving him standing there—rejected.

"Why didn't you let me kiss you that day, Antonia?" Michael asked, blunt, as if he'd been reading my mind again.

"I wasn't ready." I decided to be honest. "You caught me off guard, I was nervous, I didn't want to be just another . . ."

". . . one of all the many girls that I've kissed." Michael finished the sentence for me.

"That, too. Yes."

"Well, logic says that if I really *do* kiss all the girls who go to Holy Angels, then it will have to be your turn at some point, right?"

"Noooo," I said, sounding more sure than I felt. "We're just being friends, remember?"

"We can stop being friends when I kiss you," he said, grinning.

"News flash, Michael: I don't kiss boys who'll kiss just anybody. A kiss has to be *special*, Michael."

"What makes you think just because I've kissed a few girls that kissing you can't be special? I think there are plenty of girls who'd argue with you on that one."

"Exactly the problem. Too many."

"Hmmm. I wonder what it would be like."

126

"What?"

"Kissing Antonia Lucia Labella."

"I wouldn't know," I said before I could stop myself, trying to think of something to cover up what I'd just admitted. "I wouldn't know . . . what it's like to kiss Andy Rotellini, for example," I added, wanting to disappear when I realized that in trying to cover my blunder I'd just made another—giving Michael the information to which just moments before I'd denied him access.

"Andy Rotellini? Is *that* who you like?"

"I might kiss him if he was interested, yes," I said, since the cat was already out of the bag.

"You'd go out with Andy Rotellini over *me*?"

"Going out with you is not on the table, remember? And since, as you claimed earlier, friends tell each other things—like who they like and would go out with—then yes, if Andy asked me out, I would go out with him."

"Andy's not the type who asks girls out, Antonia. Trust me."

"And you are?"

"Whether or not you believe me, I am exactly that kind of guy," he said, defensive. "So you like Andy Rotellini," he said again, as if he couldn't believe it was true.

"Who do *you* like, while we're on the subject?"

"Wouldn't you like to know."

"Yes, as a matter of fact, I am curious," I pressed, wondering if there was any truth to what Maria overhead from Veronica, realizing that I really wanted to know because the thought of them together bothered me.

"It would be more accurate to ask who likes *me*."

"Okay. Just tell me. Who is it?"

"Your lovely cousin Veronica."

"So you and my cousin *do* have a thing going on. Maria was right. Interesting . . ." I said, trying to sound normal. Inside I was thinking I'd rather die than watch Veronica make out with Michael, flirt with Michael, and have to deal with Michael visiting her at the store while I was working.

"So what do you think? Should I go out with her?" His voice was playful, teasing.

"Um, only if you like girls who are stupid and annoying."

"Ooh. Harsh. You guys definitely don't have the family love, do you?"

"Well, she's a generally nasty person, and if you haven't noticed already, she hooks up with *everybody*, which, I guess, maybe makes her a good match for you." I couldn't resist.

"I'll ignore that comment," he said. "She's pretty in her own way, I suppose."

"Pretty ridiculous," I said, not liking this turn in our conversation, suddenly feeling drowsy again. "I *have* to go back to bed. Tomorrow I have to begin winterizing the fig trees. Besides, I don't want my mom catching us like this."

"If you insist."

"I do," I said, getting up from the chair.

"It was nice talking to you, Antonia."

"Yeah. Thanks for stopping by. Careful there, with my cousin Veronica."

"I bet you'd like it."

"Like *what*? You dating Veronica?"

"No. Kissing me. There's a lot I could teach you."

"You don't let up, do you? I am *not* going to kiss you. Good night, Michael," I said in a huff, shutting the window and turning off the light. I got back under the covers for the second time that night, willing my mind to focus on the fact that Andy Rotellini would be working at the store all the next day to help lull me to dreamland again. But my thoughts instead were captured by the hateful concept of Michael dating Veronica, and whether Michael had any idea I'd never been kissed. As I drifted off to sleep, I wondered if Michael's plan was to somehow change this fact himself.

13

I Pray to St. Walburga About the Fig-Tree Burying and Lose the Power of Speech During Andy's First Shift at the Market

My alarm blared like an angry siren at 7:00 a.m. After hitting snooze, I flung myself back against the mess of pillows and blankets, avoiding the sunlight that poured through the window across the bed. I cursed myself for staying up so late talking to Michael. I was about to doze off again when I sprang up with a start, unable to hold back a huge grin despite the early-morning hour.

How could I have forgotten?

Today was . . . ANDY ROTELLINI'S FIRST SHIFT AT LABELLA'S MARKET! The love of my life was going to be working at the store!

Granted, I'd be killing myself today over the fig trees. *But still . . .*

It felt like a pre-Thanksgiving, fig-burying miracle.

I went to my closet and gazed dreamily at the row of pleated green, yellow, and white plaid skirts on the bottom rung, below what seemed like an endless expanse of white button-downs, and shoved them aside. Today was a no-uniform day. Catholic schoolgirls always lived for the weekends, when we could break free of our standardized attire. I grabbed a pair of jeans and a long-sleeved white T-shirt to layer with my new, red T that said "Love Me" on it (hint, hint). Remembering my promise, I grabbed a bra from my underwear drawer.

"Antonia!" my mother yelled from the kitchen. "You still have to eat and help open the store before you can get going on the trees!"

"I'm coming," I practically sang, shoving my feet into tennis shoes and grabbing a jacket. Normally her reminder would have annoyed me. But for once I couldn't wait for the workday to begin. Never before had winterizing the fig trees felt so appealing.

I stopped by the bathroom to brush my teeth and take a quick look in the mirror, piling as much of my hair as I could fit into a fat silver clip. I puckered my lips in a pout, wishing I was allowed to wear lipstick.

Before leaving, I made sure to petition St. Walburga. The forecast was for sun and temperatures in the 60's, but I wasn't taking any chances.

Dear St. Walburga, O Patron Saint of Harvests, Against Storms and Coughing, though you have nothing to do with figs (technically) and I am not about to harvest anything, you are the closest saint I can think of to help (aside from

Charles, the apple man, who I am tired of asking for favors) with the out-of-control expectation that I, Antonia Lucia Labella, winterize the fig trees this weekend. Well, I suppose you could be related to the tree-burying process because if I cannot sufficiently bury the trees for the ridiculously cold winters and snowstorms we get every year, there will be no figs to harvest this spring. So I ask for your intervention in this matter. Also, speaking of storms and coughing, it would be great if it did not rain today so I don't end up soaking wet, and inevitably coughing for weeks on end, which is not only unbecoming (my face while coughing) but not at all helpful in the getting-kissed department (let's say, for example, if right before Andy Rotellini tries to kiss me in the storeroom I burst into a coughing fit because I spent all weekend stormed on while burying two trees, this would be really unfortunate). Thank you, St. Walburga, for your intercession in these matters.

I set off through the house, passing my mother—who seemed stunned that I required no further encouragement to get myself going—and disappeared down the stairs to the market before she could say another word.

I couldn't remember the last time I felt this giddy.

"Hey, Antonia," Francesca said, still half-asleep when I burst through the door, her short hair mussed on one side as if she'd just rolled out of bed herself.

"Feeling better?" My voice was cheery.

"Much," she said, plopping down on the stool behind the counter, an unspoken statement that she wasn't planning to help with the opening checklist. For once, I didn't care.

"I'm so glad to hear that. The flu is just awful. Can you hand me the 'To Do' book, please?"

"Here." Francesca reached over and handed me the notebook, making a show of what a huge effort this required.

"Let's see," I said, mostly to myself since I knew Francesca didn't care what had to get done. "Put out the pastries, straighten the tower of canned tomatoes and the shelves of olive oil, organize the torrone section." Old-worlders like my mom and all the recently immigrated Italian ladies who shopped at our store loved torrone—a nougatty, almondy Italian candy—so we carried the widest variety in all of Rhode Island.

The door jingled.

"Hey, Antonia," Andy Rotellini said, walking his beautiful self up to the counter. "Did your mother tell you that I was starting work this morning?"

He said this as if it were no big deal when it was SUCH A HUGE DEAL.

Meanwhile, I stood there frozen, the large tray of spinach pies I was about to put out held in front of me like an offering. I held my breath. I tried to think of something to say.

"Um" was all I managed during what could have been the beginning of the most important boy-interaction of my entire almost-sixteen-year career as a girl.

"What Antonia means," Francesca cut in, going from

sleepy to perky in an instant, batting her eyelashes as she sauntered over to Andy before I could do or say anything else, "is that yes, we knew you'd be here today and we're thrilled for the help. Let me show you around."

"Yeah" was word two that escaped my mouth and I nodded my head as if I approved of this tour, watching as Francesca, who flirted with everything that moved even though she was getting married in three months, directed Andy around the market. All the good feelings I'd had for her just moments before vanished. As I finally put the tray of spinach pies onto the pastry shelf, in my mind I noted that a Patron Saint of Using Your Words would have been helpful at the moment.

"And this is the stockroom," I could hear Francesca saying.

Ooh, THE STOCKROOM.

Andy would be working in the stockroom! Presumably, at least occasionally, with me! Impure thoughts began flying through my head: Andy and me in the stockroom laughing over something. Andy and me in the stockroom kissing passionately behind the canned tomatoes. Andy and me having a romantic moment in the stockroom after I've closed the market for the night and turned off the lights!

Deep breaths, I told myself, since I didn't want to get too carried away. Before laughing, kissing, and romance were possible I first had to learn to utter complete sentences in Andy's presence. This was a job for St. Teresa, the Patron Saint of Grace. I silently petitioned her:

Dear St. Teresa, I know you are busy because lots of people are in need of grace and everything, but if you could just help me have a little bit of it while I'm around Andy I'd be eternally grateful. Oh, and if you manage to remove any graceful potential from Veronica, Concetta, and Francesca when they're working at the store, that would be a huge help. No—wait. Forget that. That's not very nice. I take that last part back. Thank you, St. Teresa, for your attention.

Francesca proceeded to monopolize Andy for almost an hour, introducing him to virtually every canned vegetable and box of vermicelli we sold in the market, while I moved through the checklist, still tongue-tied. When I looked at the clock again, it was almost eight. Time to get outside. Maria would be here any minute. You knew you had a good friend when she'd show up at eight on a Saturday morning to help you bury the family fig trees. And all I needed to quell any angst about the job ahead was to recall my total joy about Andy's new position at the store, which finally put me in prime position to (a) get Andy Rotellini to really notice me and then (b) get Andy Rotellini to give me my very first, totally amazing, dreamy, passionate kiss! If only I could figure out how to talk in his presence. Maybe *when* he kissed me this could count as my Miracle Number One on the road to sainthood. It certainly seemed to require a miracle to get yourself kissed—at least at the right time and with the right boy.

"Antonia! Time to get going!" my mother yelled from upstairs.

Perhaps it would help with the kissing if I was beatified (i.e., beautified) by the Vatican first.

Despite my reluctance to leave Francesca alone in the market with Andy, I knew I had to get to work outside. Before my mother could yell my name again, I was in my jacket and out the door to the yard in back, soothed by the knowledge that Andy would be nearby the entire day.

14

It's Raining Men While Maria and I Are Busy Pruning

Hi, Antonia," said a male voice, but not the one I'd been hoping to hear. Andy was just steps away and yet he hadn't come out once to say hello or to offer his assistance.

"Hi, Michael," I yelled from my perch on the ladder, squinting in the bright sun, trying not to be fazed by his arrival. Instead, I concentrated on the branch I was about to clip with shears big enough to chop down a small tree. As I squeezed the handle, there was a loud *snap* and the branch broke free, tumbling down against the lower limbs and onto the grass below. "Hey, can you make yourself useful and gather those branches down there?" I called out.

"I've got it, Antonia," Maria said, emerging from behind the other tree, where she'd been pruning its lower limbs.

"Hey, Michael," she said, giving him a wave. Maria and I had been working steadily all morning and I hadn't even had a chance to brief her about my nighttime rendezvous with Michael—though I did manage to get some delighted squeals in about seeing Andy.

"Looks like you already have excellent help," Michael said, approaching the bottom of the ladder.

"Haven't seen you in a while," I lied. "So are you going to just stand there or what?"

A big smile spread across Michael's face.

"Wait. Don't answer that. I don't want to know," I said, feeling that familiar head rush I always got when we locked eyes, which made me consider climbing down from the ladder so I didn't plummet to my death. Death by fig-tree winterization was all I needed today of all days. Though I probably had a better chance of becoming the Patron Saint of Figs and Fig Trees if I died on their behalf. And as appealing as this possibility of sainthood was, I reminded myself that (a) my goal was to become a living saint, (b) I refused to live up to my name saint and become yet another fifteen-year-old dead virgin named Antonia, and (c) I really should get down because not only was I getting dizzy but I was currently giving Michael an unobstructed view of my butt.

"How about I come up there and join you?" Michael asked.

"That answer is definitely no," I said, carefully stepping from rung to rung until I reached the ground, still grasping the pruning shears as if they were a weapon to keep Michael at bay.

"That was nice of you to give Antonia a ride yesterday,"

Maria said, emerging again from underneath the other tree, wiping her brow. We were sweating from the hard labor.

"Anytime, Maria."

"I'm sure, Michael," Maria said with a knowing laugh.

Michael looked from me to Maria and upward to the two towering trees that left little room for much else, and back to me with skepticism on his face. The Labella fig trees *were* unusually big.

"This is quite a job," he said.

"We can handle it," I said. Though, not without serious assistance. Tomorrow we'd have half the neighborhood men here to help bend the top branches to the ground, holding them while Gram, Mom, and I secured them with rope into small mountains of cardboard and canvas.

"You really know how to make a guy feel welcome, Antonia." Michael's eyes moved to the pruning shears I was still holding out as if I were about to attack him.

"Someone has to ward off the throng of guys looking for Maria," I said, lowering the shears to my side.

"Oh, please," Maria said. "My heart is already taken."

"So I've heard," Michael said. "John Cronin, eh? Taming a popular senior like him is quite an accomplishment."

"He *is* amazing, isn't he?"

"Just be careful. He gets around, Maria."

"Like you don't, Michael," Maria came back, laughing.

"I'm saving myself for Antonia," Michael said. Our conversation last night came back in a rush. I felt my face flush as red as my T-shirt.

"Right. Mabye I should go back to my tree and leave you two alone," Maria said, backing away.

"Don't go, Maria," I said, half laughing, half pleading. "I have no idea what he's talking about."

"Of course you do, Antonia. Just last night you were saying how I kiss all the HA girls and I was saying how I hadn't kissed—"

"Need some help?" said another voice before Michael could finish, and I couldn't stop the smile that spread across my face. Finally! Andy Rotellini was standing in the back doorway of the market looking *godly* in perfect-fitting jeans and a white T-shirt that set off the bronze color of his skin. I suddenly found it impossible to utter another syllable. "Your grandmother said I might be more useful out here than in the market this afternoon."

"Hi, Andy," Maria called out since I wasn't showing any sign of language skills. "Of course you know Michael because you're in the same class, or should I make an introduction?" Maria looked amused by the unusual overflow of eligible men in my vicinity.

"Hey, Mike. What's up?" Andy and Michael did the requisite guy-nod-hello gesture.

"Yeah. Hi. Andy," I managed to croak, the tiny space in the yard that wasn't occupied by the trees suddenly feeling overcrowded with Michael, Andy, and me all standing there together. The laughter left Michael's eyes and I found myself wishing Michael would decide to leave. I'd been waiting for a chance to get to know Andy forever and that chance was finally here, but so was Michael. "We'd love your help, Andy," I said, giving him a belated answer. I wanted to fix this awkward situation. "Which also means you, Michael, are off the hook for fig-tree duty since my mother is actually *paying* Andy to be here. Today is his first day working at the store. Had I mentioned that he'd be working here?" Michael should understand. We did just have a conversation about the fact that I had a thing for Andy Rotellini.

"I was just going, actually," Michael replied. I didn't have to look to know he was hurt—it was there in his voice. "I told Veronica I'd pay her a visit this afternoon anyway."

"You did?" I tried to sound nonchalant. "That's great, I mean," I said, crossing the small patch of grass between me and the ladder without looking at Michael. "Why wait? I mean, go see her now so you guys can have lunch. Though, you might want to pick something up from the market on your way since Veronica is not the best cook and neither is her mother." I grabbed the shears and climbed back up, rung by rung, reminding myself that I didn't have time to socialize. I began hacking at one of the thicker branches, barely paying attention to what I was doing.

"Thanks for the advice, Antonia." I heard Michael behind me. "Maria. Andy." Michael said his goodbyes. "I'll be seeing you. Nice chatting."

The gate clicked shut and Michael was gone before anyone had the chance to say anything else.

"So, Antonia? What would you like me to do?" I'd almost forgotten that Andy, the love of my life, was still standing there, awaiting direction.

"Um. Well." I tried to say something intelligible.

"Let me get you a pair of clipping shears and then Antonia will show you how to prune the lower branches," Maria said, heading over to Andy, rescuing me.

I stared at Andy, watched him standing there at my house, gorgeous as ever, something I'd wanted for what seemed like forever, and I wanted to believe that in that moment Andy captivated me all over again. But the truth was I couldn't stop thinking about Michael. And Veronica. The thought of them together didn't feel right. A knot began growing in my stomach, and I wasn't at all confident that Andy's presence could make it disappear.

15

I Confront My Mother About Her Nonexistent Dating Life and I Experience Tragic Vatican Rejection

It was Sunday night. The big weekend was over and I was kneeling before the tiny portrait of St. Walburga that leaned against my vanity mirror. She was standing, eyes facing the ground, holding a scepter in one hand and three ears of corn in the other.

Dear St. Walburga, O Patron Saint of Harvests, Against Storms and Coughing, even though you technically have nothing to do with figs or fig trees, I thank you for watching over us this weekend in what was a very successful fig-tree burying. Not only are the family trees — which are basically the family treasures — protected for yet another cold Rhode Island winter, but the sun shined on us for two entire days, not only keeping me from coming down with a cold followed by potentially obstructive and unfortunately timed coughing fits (such as when my beloved is about to kiss me, which he will eventually), but also providing a warm weather incen-

tive for the neighbors to come out and help with the burying after Sunday Mass. It was a community effort, not to mention the perfect opportunity for some of the men to flirt with my mother, who is so in need of a date. Thank you, St. Walburga, for your intercession in these matters.

I struck a match to light the candle I'd placed nearby. I sank into the red, cushioned vanity chair with its old-fashioned, heart-shaped metal back, and watched my reflection flicker in the light.

I imagined my mother sitting here in this very chair—back when the vanity used to be hers—fixing her hair, putting on jewelry, getting ready to go out with my father for the first time when she was my age. Maybe after Dad died she'd decided she had no more use for it, that her evenings out were in the past. Or maybe she just couldn't bear to look at it anymore, because of all the memories it brought back. So she gave it to me. I hated to think about how lonely she must be, but she refused to date any of the neighborhood bachelors. I wondered whether she'd loosen up with me if she started going out with someone. I had even brought up the subject at dinner earlier in the evening.

Mom, Gram, and I were celebrating the fig-burying, clinking glasses of Asti Spumanti, when I decided to pop the question.

"Mom," I began, cautious, knowing I was about to dive into forbidden territory. We were sitting around the kitchen table, with its red-checked vinyl tablecloth. Tall candles radiated a soft glow over everything. Gram had thrown together a sauce and we were having it over linguini. Mom had even set out the nice china and crystal. Everyone seemed so happy. "I was wondering if you ever thought of going out with someone from the neighborhood."

"What are you talking about, Antonia? I go out with Sister Aideen for breakfast the first and third Tuesdays of every month, and I go to the Italian Women in Business lunch every other week to see the girls." She rolled linguini onto her fork with the help of a spoon. She avoided eye contact.

"No, I meant with a *man*. *On a date*."

"I'm too old to date," she said, taking a big swig from her wineglass. "Besides, I love your father."

"Mom, you are only forty, which is so *not* too old." She might drive me crazy, but I couldn't deny that my mother was still beautiful. "Just because you go out with someone doesn't mean you don't love Dad anymore," I added, nervous that I was pushing too far.

"I'm not interested in dating," my mother said. "End of topic."

"Mr. D'Agostino was totally flirting with you when he was helping you tie up the canvas." I'd decided to press my luck since she hadn't yet yelled or thrown any plates.

"Antonia's right, sweetheart, and he's a cute one, that Giuseppe," Gram chimed in. "You are my beautiful daughter and I want you to be happy." She leaned over and gave my mom a kiss on the cheek.

"Ma," my mother said, glaring back at Gram. "Leave me alone. Nobody was flirting with anybody and I'm not dating. I love your father," she said again.

"I love him, too," I said in a hush. "And if you are worried about what I'd think, I'm telling you now that I think it's a great idea. And this isn't the first time Mr. D'Agostino has acted this way around you," I forged on. "He stays forever talking to you when he comes into the store. I bet if you stopped wearing black every day, he might ask you out. I think he likes you." I closed my eyes, hoping for the best. "And I think you might like him too."

"Antonia Lucia Labella!" My mother dropped her fork and it clattered noisily against the plate. The steam from the pasta rose around her face in a mist. "Mind your own business!" She downed the last of her Asti Spumanti, and stormed off to her room, slamming the door.

And *that* was the happy end to our celebratory family dinner.

I got up from the vanity and grabbed my Saint Diary off the nightstand. I figured it was time for another saint specialization brainstorming session.

"Sweetheart?" Gram's excited voice was outside my door. "Can I come in?"

"Sure, Gram," I replied.

The look on her face was eager.

"A letter came for you yesterday," she began, taking out the long, paper-thin envelope that was sticking out of her sweater pocket. "Special delivery. I figured I'd wait until you got through all the hoopla this weekend to give it to you."

"Is it from . . ." My voice trailed off when I noticed the airmail stamp.

"It's from the Vatican," she whispered, her voice reverent.

"Wow," I said, taking the letter from her hand.

"I love you, sweetheart." She leaned over, giving me a squeeze. I could smell the Oil of Olay she always put on her skin. She swore it kept her young.

Seeing the official Vatican seal across the envelope flap gave me a thrill. But it was soon followed by a wave of anxiety. This could be it. This could be the letter informing me that *I*, Antonia Lucia Labella, of Providence, Rhode Island, was to be the new Patron Saint of Figs!

Or, that I *wasn't*.

I cut through the top of the envelope with a letter opener, careful to preserve the seal, and removed the delicate paper inside. I unfolded it and began to read.

My heart sank. It was a form letter—a short one—dated November 15, which meant my follow-up e-mail from Friday hadn't mattered one bit.

Antonia Lucia Labella
Labella's Market of Federal Hill
33 Atwells Avenue
Providence, RI USA

November 15

Dear Miss Labella:

Thank you very much for your letter regarding the need for a Patron Saint of Figs. We receive many requests and, due to the volume, cannot respond to all of them. If at any point in the future we decide to name a saint for figs or the fig tree, we will be sure to inform you.

While we welcome your suggestions for possible patron saints, please recall that, though in very rare cases we have fast-tracked a person (e.g., Mother Teresa) to sainthood upon time of death, generally there is a five-year postmortem waiting period before we can start the beatification process.

Blessings in Christ,
The Vatican Committee on Sainthood
Vatican City
Rome
ITALY

I sat down on my bed, blinking back the tears. My years of reaching out about sainthood to Pope Gregory XVII felt suddenly futile, a childish effort carried on too long.

"Antonia?" Gram was still standing there, waiting, patient. She didn't even have to ask what the letter said. "It's okay, sweetheart. There's always a next time, you know. I believe in you. Your father did, too."

I heard her tiptoe out of the room, shutting the door behind her. Tears spilled down my cheeks.

For the first time ever I took what would normally be a precious correspondence—a letter from the Vatican—

crumpled it up, and threw it across the room. It hit the closet door and fell to the floor.

Usually I didn't take rejection this hard, but maybe this was one rejection too many. Maybe I wasn't really cut out for sainthood after all.

There was a rapping on my bedroom window, which I ignored. I knew it was Michael but I couldn't talk to him right now, didn't want to talk to anyone. I felt relieved that I'd pulled the shade down tight earlier. He was probably mad at me about this weekend anyway, and I had no desire to make amends at the moment. I waited, silent, still as a statue, until the rapping stopped, until I heard the faint sounds of Michael climbing back down the fire escape.

I wiped away the tears from my face, and thought of my father. Thinking of him gave me courage. The thing I loved most about being Catholic was that for Catholics, the dead, the saintly, were all still with us, among us, so present we could talk to them as if they were still here. And miracles happened all the time—the world was full of them. Mom, Dad, *and* Gram all taught me that. And Mrs. Bevalaqua was living proof.

A tiny smile crept onto my face.

One miracle. That's all it took for beatification. I *knew* it was possible.

But *how*? I sighed, knowing I still wasn't ready to give up on my quest, knowing that the first step was always the hardest.

PART 2

The Patron Saint of People Who Make Pasta

Vatican Committee on Sainthood
Vatican City
Rome, Italy

December 1

To Whom It May Concern (ideally the Pope if he's available):

As a Catholic in good standing and a frequent venerator of saints, I was shocked to learn that of the over 5,000 (!!) saints named in the last couple millennia, there has yet to be a saint for people who make pasta. I mean, there are patron saints for people ridiculed for piety, people who are unattractive, and even people who fight against communism. (Is that supposed to be for America, by the way? You could be more explicit. We all know who you mean.) I am pretty convinced that if we can have a patron saint for people who fight against communism (i.e., the overzealous U.S. government), we are certainly due a saint for us little people who fight to make pasta on the home front. I mean, if you're not careful with how much water you add to the dough, let me tell you, you'll have a battle on your hands when you try to roll it out. And the flour! It gets everywhere. We're talking all over the house, in your hair, on your clothes. A Patron Saint of People Who Make Pasta would be useful in so many ways: for helping with flour removal (have you ever tried to get flour out of your favorite black T-shirt?), for adding water (you measure in halves of eggshells. Eggshells! At least in my family. Try cracking eggs just the right size. Different every time, I tell you), and for preventing the dough from sticking to the rolling pin (you may as well throw the whole batch out at that point). I am convinced that by naming a Patron Saint of People Who Make Pasta, you could have another St. Anthony on your hands—in other words, this saint would have instant popularity. Wouldn't that be fantastic?

Thank you for your attention to this matter.

Blessings,
Antonia Lucia Labella
Labella's Market of Federal Hill
33 Atwells Avenue
Providence, RI USA
saint2b@live.com

P.S. To help the process move along smoothly, I'd be happy to offer myself up as this much needed object of devotion for Catholic pasta makers everywhere. (By the way, I meant to ask, were you able to open that JPG file I sent last month? If you need a higher-res version, or a TIF file, let me know.) Hope to hear from you soon!

16

Mom, Gram, and I Prepare for the Feast
of St. Lucia, and I Pray to St. Augustine,
the Saint Who Once Loved Sex, About Andy

I poured the contents of an entire bag of flour onto the
wooden counter, worn smooth from years of use. I
shaped the silky pile into a mountain of soft, white powder
until my hands reached all the way around, as if I were
pulling the flour into a strange hug. Tiny specks of white
hung in the air. I watched them fall, settling onto the pile,
the counter, the floor. My dark hair.

"What are you waiting for, Antonia? A new pope,
Madonna?"

"I was thinking about how I hope I don't fall asleep in
school today," I said, not looking up. I knew my mother
was watching me from the stove while she gave the sauce a
turn. It was early Friday morning, December 9, before
school.

"When I was your age I got up at four a.m. to help with
the cooking every day *and* I got straight A's," she said
in her let-me-now-lecture-Antonia tone, pausing to take a

taste from the wooden spoon. She gave a few loud, scraping turns to the pepper mill and added another leaf of basil. "But then I married your father and didn't have to worry about school anymore. Just the cooking."

"Thanks for the feminist words of wisdom, Ma," I said, sliding my hands around the base of the flour until it became a circular wall. "That's really helpful advice seeing that I'm planning on getting married next year."

"Don't get smart with me, Antonia, and you're getting flour everywhere! It's spilling onto the floor," my mother yelled as she moved away from the stovetop, stooping to stare into my eyes so that I was forced to look back. She glared at the sticky mass beginning to take shape in front of me, and then returned to the pasta dough she was kneading.

Gram, Mom, and I had been lined up in a row, spread across the long wooden counter in the center of our kitchen for most of the morning, each working our own pasta-making station. Despite the kitchen chaos, my mother's apron, sweater, pants, and dark hair were all spotless, as if she hadn't yet lifted a single spice or even touched a tomato. I, on the other hand, had spatters of red all down my pajama top and flour in my hair.

There had never been a greater need for a Patron Saint of People Who Make Pasta. I'd wiped all memories of November's fig failure clear from my mind. It wasn't smart to be too sentimental in the business of proposing new saint specializations. I concentrated on the sticky dough in my hands.

It took all the women in the house to get ready for the big celebration that we were hosting that night. Like every other year, we were about to observe the feast of St. Lucia. The entire neighborhood would squeeze into our apartment to enjoy the food we'd been up at four a.m. preparing for nine days straight, especially the pastas.

Everyone would be there. Including Andy!

And Michael, too. We were actually trying the friends thing. Though being friends with Michael seemed to require that we spend almost as much time together as I spent with Maria.

"Antonia! Stop using so much flour or your raviolis are going to sink like rocks, and then we won't have enough for everybody and it will be a disaster. *Madonna!*"

"This dough will be fine," I said, trying to ease the drama erupting from my mother. She was never more stressed than on the day of the big party each year. "I know it won't be as good as yours, *Mother*, but then nobody's is." I wasn't above flattery. "And besides, we already have enough to feed all of Federal Hill."

In addition to the mountains of food we'd prepared— the linguini with clams, the squid-ink pasta for the seafood, the broccoli penne, the braciola, the meatballs, the six different sauces, each one for its own variety of pasta, the lasagnas, raviolis, raviolinis, and tortellinis filled with cheeses and meats, the chicken cutlets, the eggplant parmigiana, the steamed Italian-style artichokes, the salads, and, of course, the out-of-control range of cookies, zeppoli, and other confections—like every other year as far back as I could remember, I would be providing one of the evening's central entertainments. I had the dubious honor of playing St. Lucia. The irony of getting to be saint for a day was not lost on me. Unfortunately, becoming Lucia required that I wear a crown of lit candles on my head, risking not only life and limb but my entire head of hair. I not so fondly nicknamed St. Lucia the Patron Saint of Fire Hazards. Should I end up bald after the evening's walk of fire, I suspected it might put a damper on all the attention Andy had been paying me lately.

Andy had been coming around. Literally. He was working at the market three times a week—far too little if you ask me. He still didn't talk much, but I kept catching him staring at me with meaningful looks. Even in church at Our Lady of Loreto!

There I was last Sunday, minding my own business in the family pew, leafing through the hymnal while Father Bernardino droned on with his homily about what, I had no idea. I decided to do a little pre-Communion-line people watching. That was the best part about going to Mass: looking around to see who else was there, especially during Communion, when everyone was filing up to the front. I always made sure to sit by the aisle for optimal viewing.

I was ever-so-inconspicuously glancing around the church to see who was there—Maria and family: *check*; Michael McGinnis and family: *check*—when I noticed Andy just a few rows back. ANDY ROTELLINI AND

FAMILY: *CHECK!* That's when I also noticed that *he* was gazing *lovingly* back at *me*! At least, that was how I saw it. And before I turned away, *he smiled.*

ANDY ROTELLINI SMILED AT ME in a house of God!

Unfortunately, Gram, Veronica, and Concetta, who, like me, were also looking around, noticed this miraculous event, too. And so did Michael. When I noticed Michael noticing me noticing Andy, there was—I don't know—jealousy on his face? He'd been coming by my window almost every other night, but all we'd talk about was whether or not he should go out with my stupid cousin or he would listen to my analysis of every glance and one-syllable word Andy had given me since we'd last talked about Andy's previous glances and one-syllable words.

Anyway, I sat there, blushing but trying to look cool, glancing through the *Glory and Praise to Our God* songbook, while at the same time I wanted to shout, "TAKE ME NOW, ANDY! I don't care if Father Bernardino is transubstantiating the bread and the wine!" That was when Veronica leaned toward me.

"So you like Andy Rotellini, do you?" she whispered in my ear, so close I could feel the crunch of her moussed-up hair against my cheek. "Too bad your mother won't let you out of the house at night."

Veronica slid back in the pew. I could hear her and Concetta laughing.

Then Gram leaned over from my other side and whispered, "He's a nice Italian Catholic boy, Antonia. Good for you."

Which made me go red in the face.

There were three types of Catholics who lived in Providence: the Italian, the Irish, and the Portuguese. We Italians lived on Federal Hill, the Irish congregated in South Providence, and the Portuguese were scattered everywhere in between. In my mother's era it would have been scandalous for, let's say, an Italian-Catholic to marry a Portuguese-Catholic. It wasn't enough that both were Catholic, they had to be from the same "people," too. Not so much with my generation. Though, if one day I came home with a non-Italian boy, my mother would definitely get the rosary out. Maybe she'd even say a novena—a nine-day prayer ritual you performed only when you needed some *serious* Trinitarian intervention.

The Italians, the Portuguese, and the Irish—we all came together for Mass at Our Lady of Loreto though, where, I should mention in yet another act of painful self-revelation, my family had donated the statue of *The* Virgin (you know—*that* Virgin) in *my name* in honor of my birth. It was unveiled at my baptism. Mom and Dad had brought over the stone from Italy. Spared no expense. We were always pinching pennies but somehow could afford to ship a block of marble over from the homeland. Ever since I was old enough to "appreciate" this gesture I'd worried that having my name immortalized under the Immaculate One had done permanent damage to my chances of ever becoming un-immaculate. Between my name saint and my Virgin statue, I seemed destined for eternal purity.

Though, it was very possible that Andy Rotellini's LUSTFUL STARES were breaking down the stronghold that Mother Mary and St. Antonia—the virgin-until-death—had on me.

"Stop adding so much flour, Antonia," my mother barked again, yanking me out of my happy last-Sunday memories.

"Sure, Mom." I sighed, closing my eyes while working what had become a pillowy ball of pasta dough, back and forth, from hand to hand, on my section of the counter, while still conjuring up images of Andy in my mind: Andy's tall, muscular figure, reaching to place cans of tomato paste high up on one of the market shelves; Andy coming through the front door to start his shift, walking up to me as I sat, transfixed, at the front counter watching; Andy turning to me, staring with those gorgeous dark eyes, to ask whether he should put out the new bulbs of garlic that just arrived . . . Any day now he was going to move beyond one-word greetings and inquiries about garlic displays to professing his undying love for me, explaining how he could not go even another second without KISSING ME PASSIONATELY!

I decided to petition St. Augustine for the second time that morning and the tenth time that month with what was now a familiar prayer on my and Andy's behalf. Of *all* the saints, I'd decided that St. Augustine would know how to respond, like no other virginal saint before or after him, to one of my Andy requests. After all, St. Augustine was famous for praying, "Lord, make me chaste, but not just yet!" because he loved loving women so much he wasn't quite ready to give up his favorite activity for fame, power, and his future life of celibacy. He eventually had to, of course, in order to become the bishop people remember him as and make his mother happy by being a good Christian boy after her, like, thirty-year record of praying for his conversion — but he did so *begrudgingly*.

O St. Augustine, I know you are really the Patron Saint of Brewers; Printers; Kalamazoo, Michigan; and Sore Eyes, and not even close to anything resembling the Patron Saint of Love, Matchmaking, or Kissing (among other possible sexy activities). This is despite the fact that you loved all that stuff at one point in your life (I mean, you waited until you were thirty-two to give up women, and even then you were pretty sorrowful about it all), which is why I am putting all my hope and trust that you of all saints will understand that it will indeed be a SIGHT FOR SORE EYES (mine, that is) to see Andy Rotellini standing before me, above me, or anywhere in my near vicinity, ready to pounce on yours truly, Antonia Lucia Labella, in an act of amorous attention! And speaking of eyes, which is your specialty, mine are practically falling out at this point from all the strain of mustering lust-filled looks for Andy Rotellini's benefit anytime he happens to glance in my direction. I suggest you hark back to your wayward youth, pick out a fondly remembered encounter—you know what I'm talking about—and relive vicariously through me! Isn't that a great idea? Thank you, St. Augustine, for your attention to this matter.

"Antonia! What are you doing?" My mother interrupted my sexy request, pulling me out of my trance. A thick white cloud rose from the floor. "O *Madonna*, what a mess! Pay attention to what you are doing!"

The big bag of flour sitting on the counter where I'd been working the dough was no longer there. I must have knocked it over.

"Um, sorry. I don't know what happened," I said, staring at the mountainous powdery mess.

"Don't give me you don't know what happened. You weren't careful is what happened."

"I'll clean it up," I said, setting the dough aside to wash my hands and deal with the spill, thinking that this was definitely not the best way to start off the feast day of St. Lucia.

"I'll help you, sweetheart," Gram offered.

"No, Gram. I can do it. I don't want you bending down on the floor."

"You're right, *you'll* clean it up. What a waste! I just opened that bag of flour, too," my mother muttered. "Watch where you step! *Madonna!* What's wrong with you this morning?"

Another cloud puffed up around me. I'd walked right into the slippery white pile on my way to the sink. Sighing,

I turned on the faucet to scrape away the dough caked to my fingers, and made one last plea to St. Augustine:

St. Augustine, of all days, today would be the day to come through for me here on the Andy matter. It's the feast of St. Lucia in our house after all! I need something to look forward to right now and I really *don't want to go down in history as St. Antonia, the girl who not only died making pasta but did so a virgin without so much as a kiss!*

O Madonna.

17

The Unthinkable Happens

After what seemed like forever, the floor was spotless. I was covered in sweat and flour, and the curls that escaped my ponytail were plastered against the side of my face.

"Antonia," my mother snapped. "I need you to go down to the storeroom and get another bag of flour. One of the big ones. As big as the one you *spilled*."

"Yes, Mom," I said, looking up at the old grandfather clock hanging on the wall. It was barely a quarter past six. This morning was never going to end. I still had almost two full hours before I left for school. I did my best to clean my flour-covered arms and legs with a dry dish towel.

"Antonia! What are you waiting for? The guests to arrive tonight?"

"Calm down, Ma," I said. "I'm going."

I slipped my feet into my sparkly red flip-flops and

trudged down the stairs, shoving the heavy wooden door to the market at the bottom with my hip. A wedge of light grew wider as it swung open. Someone was either in the market or had left the lights on last night. I stepped onto the black concrete floor and stopped. The aisles were dark. Only the lights by the front counter and from inside the storeroom were on.

"Hello . . ." I called out.

What if we're being robbed? I felt a surge of panic and called on Nicholas of Myra, Patron Saint Against Robberies and Robbers, for his protection should there be a burglar in the storeroom, stocking up on imported olive oil, garlic salt, and amaretto extract, waiting to attack the next unsuspecting virgin who happened along. I grabbed a bottle of balsamic vinegar from a nearby shelf and prepared to break it over his head.

"Hello?" I shouted, louder now, moving toward the door to the storeroom, feeling the protection from St. Nicholas surging through my pajama-clad self.

"Hey," said a voice that was music to my ears, that washed all burglar-induced fears away with a surge of adrenaline and made my heart race in an altogether different way. Andy Rotellini appeared, bathed in the heavenly glow of the light behind him. His baggy jeans hung low against his waist and his T-shirt fit his body perfectly, just enough to show off his muscular baseball-pitcher arms.

"Hi, Andy," I said, trying to maintain my composure, though I was screaming inside, Take me! TAKE ME

NOW! You know you want me! Three cheers for St. Augustine!

"Antonia?"

HE SAID MY NAME!

"Yes," I said, attempting a breathy come-hither tone.

"Why the giant bottle of balsamic vinegar raised above your head?"

"Oh. Um." I lowered the bottle, placing it on a nearby shelf packed with cans of minestrone. "I wasn't sure if . . . I mean . . . the light was on . . . I wasn't expecting anybody . . . What *are* you doing here now anyway?"

"Your mother asked me to come in before school so I could double-check the stuff for tonight."

"Yes. Of course." As usual, I'd lost the power of intelligent speech.

He leaned against the door frame, all casual, his eyes boring into me. "I was going to come upstairs when I finished. You know, to tell your mom everything was all set. Maybe see if you were around."

HE LOVES ME! He was going to SEE IF I WAS AROUND!

I attempted a nonchalant this-is-so-no-big-deal pose and instead ended up sending several cans of navy beans crashing to the floor. "Whatever. I'll get those later." I tried to act like I wasn't embarrassed by my lack of coordination.

"Yeah. Sure," he said, returning to his one-word self.

"Does my mother know you're here?" I asked, thinking, PLEASE, NO. Please don't let her know the love of my life is alone and conversing with me in the market.

"She didn't give me a specific time—just that I should get everything done before school," Andy said. "I just let myself in." He looked as if he were waiting for me to do something. "You want to keep me company awhile?" He gestured behind him into the storeroom.

"I can't stay," I said, but I was thinking, YES! YES! I am finally having a moment alone with Andy Rotellini! Who cares that it is only six-thirty in the morning, that I have a total bed-head and am unshowered, dusted from top to bottom in flour, and wearing my pajamas? Originally I'd pictured something more romantic: We'd meet up by the swing set one evening, like with Maria and John. He'd push me really high. We'd laugh. He'd declare his undying love. But I wasn't picky. I ducked past him into the storeroom, almost fainting from his nearness, and took refuge by a case of instant polenta. "My mother expects me back up in the kitchen soon," I added, managing a smile.

Andy faced me and gave me THE STARE, the same lusty I'm-a-man-of-few-words-but-who-needs-words stare, that I'd come to love lately. A look that turned my legs into TOMATO PASTE.

Without another word he walked toward me and stopped. We had never been this close and I felt small next to his tall frame. He leaned toward me, placing one hand against the wall for balance and running the other down the length of my bare arm. My skin tingled. His fingers lingered on the back of my hand.

I had to remember to breathe.

Andy Rotellini was TOUCHING ME. I was BEING TOUCHED BY A BOY.

I stared into his eyes, not knowing what to say or do.

And I waited. I waited for him to say any one of the following things:

> I've dreamed so long about this moment.
>
> I can't live another minute without you.
>
> You are the most beautiful girl I've ever laid eyes on.
>
> No one else compares to you, Antonia.
>
> I've been hoping for time alone with you ever since my first day at the market.
>
> Or even:
>
> Do you know where your mother keeps the canned artichoke hearts?

Anything. ANYTHING!

But he offered none of the above and so I consoled myself with the knowledge that Andy was quiet and mysterious, which was all part of the attraction. I decided that his dark, yearning eyes said all I'd hoped for without the need of actual words. I should have mentioned to St. Augustine that some romantic talk would have been nice.

I couldn't have everything.

Besides, at the moment, Andy's fingers were running back up my arm, over my shoulder, lingering by the strap of my tank top, playing with it, under it, over it, his eyes still on mine. I felt my face flush and was suddenly grateful I'd decided to wear a bra even under my pajamas at night. My tank top was practically see-through.

It was as if I were in a dream. Like none of this was real.

His index finger traced my collarbone.

I gasped.

AND THAT WAS WHEN IT HAPPENED. Andy's mouth, ever-so-slightly, began moving toward mine. IT WAS THE MOMENT I'D BEEN WAITING FOR MY ENTIRE LIFE. Well, aside from the Vatican declaring me a saint.

I closed my eyes and parted my lips just like Maria told me to, and waited for our mouths to meet in a delicious kiss. Any second now . . .

Then, suddenly, rather than feeling Andy's lips on mine, I felt them near MY LEFT BOOB! Right where my tank top dipped in the middle! He pressed his body hard against mine in what I would call a rather FORWARD way, while his other hand made its way up under my shirt! WHO IN THE WORLD DECIDES TO BOOB-KISS A GIRL BEFORE HE LIP-KISSES HER? WHO?

Apparently Andy Rotellini, the love of my life for the last two years!

All my hopes and dreams were dashed in a single moment.

When I finally found my voice, my bearings, I yelled, "Get off of me!" which was easy since my mouth was SO

UNOCCUPIED. I shoved Andy with all my might, using so much force that he staggered back, causing a tall stack of boxed capellini to come crashing down. "What the hell are you doing?" I was fuming.

"But you want me, Antonia . . ." he answered in what he must have thought was a sexy voice, and I might have once thought was sexy myself, but now just sounded offensive. "You've wanted me forever, Antonia. Don't think I didn't know," he said. The shock of rejection began to register on his face.

"Did you ever think of checking with me first?" I sputtered, moving away from the wall so he couldn't pin me again, wondering how I could have believed that the boy with no words was somehow a gentleman.

"I didn't need to. I just *knew*," Andy said, backing away.

"You just *knew*," I jeered. I felt cheated. "You just *knew* what?"

"There are plenty of other girls lining up to be with me who will do anything, anywhere, whenever I want," Andy said, bending down to pick up the boxes of capellini strewn across the floor.

"And you just assumed I was one of *those girls*."

"Your loss, Antonia."

"*My* loss?" I felt dizzy with disappointment. It wasn't supposed to be like this! All those romantic scenarios I'd imagined for years—all for nothing. All for a guy who clearly had never before and still did not see or respect me for who I really was, who regarded me as just one of the "plenty of other girls lining up" to be with him. What I had interpreted as mysterious, shy, and quiet was really just self-importance and vapidity.

"You just missed out on the best thing you could ever hope for, Andy Rotellini. Make sure to cross me off your girls-in-waiting lineup," I spat, dashing out of the store-room and back up the stairs.

It was suddenly clear what I needed to do, what *must* be done. I'd had a vision—maybe from God, maybe from bumping my head against that shelf of canned artichokes after shoving Andy Rotellini away—regardless, it didn't matter. My mind was racing, my body urged on by a new sense of mission: to protect unkissed girls everywhere from heartbreaking scenarios like the one I was just subjected to by the now FORMER love of my life, Andy Rotellini.

Stupid, horny St. Augustine. I took the stairs two at a time.

I had pressing Vatican business to attend to.

18

I Draft an Emergency Saint Proposal, and Get in Gram's Car, Risking Life and Limb

W hat took you so long? And where's the bag of flour?"

I dashed through the flurry of activity in the kitchen, ignoring my mother's confusion, her protests, and the concerned look from Gram, who must have noticed my disheveled state.

"Antonia?" Gram asked, worried.

"Antonia!" My mother yelled, angry.

When I reached my room I threw open the door, and let it slam shut behind me. I turned the lock. Grabbing a pen, paper, and my Saint Diary from the nightstand, I flung myself onto my bed, took a deep breath, and tried to calm down. I didn't know whether to sob or be thankful I'd found out that Andy Rotellini was a total *mascalzone* (that means "jerk-face" in Italian, more or less) before two *more* years of loving devotion from yours truly, or, even worse—marriage! I'd wasted all this time on a guy who had to be THE LEAST ROMANTIC PERSON IN THE ENTIRE UNIVERSE.

Our love affair was over before it even started.

"You come out *now*, Antonia Lucia Labella!" My mother was banging on the door with her fist.

"Leave me alone," I shouted. For once I didn't care if she was mad. I had more important things to think about.

"Antonia!"

"Go AWAY!"

"She used to be such a good girl when she was small." My mother was grumbling loud enough that I could hear her through the door. "They grow up and they are like aliens."

Who in the world thought boob-kissing a girl before mouth-kissing her was acceptable? Other than Andy Rotellini, the most obvious person who came to mind was St. Augustine! You'd think the former fourth-century Don Juan would know better—what women liked and all. When I mentioned that business about "amorous attention" and wanting to see Andy before me "ready to pounce" in all my petitions, I didn't mean it *literally*. All I wanted was a little kiss. Clearly, Augustine was not the saint to petition for all your kissing needs. There wasn't any saint for this sort of thing—not *yet*, at least—which was *exactly* why what I was about to propose to the Vatican was essential to the well-being of Catholic girls like me the world over. And probably the boys, too.

I picked up my pen and began to write:

Vatican Committee on Sainthood
Vatican City
Rome, Italy

December 9

To Whom It May Concern (ideally the Pope if he's available):

I'm writing to inform you of a *grave* oversight in the area of patron saint specializations, to replace my earlier letter this month about a Patron Saint of People Who Make Pasta, which I ask that you just file away for the time being. Though this is not to say that pasta making isn't important, since I, of all people, daughter of the most famous pasta maker in the state of Rhode Island, should know (that's Labella's Pasta, in case you were wondering or want to place an order since we ship everywhere). But there are more pressing matters at hand than pasta. Dire even!

Like the fact that, as yet, there is no Patron Saint of the Kiss, and, to be more specific, the First Kiss! I ask you: how is this possible? Young Catholic girls and boys everywhere are in DANGER, not only because of the Vatican's general need of a reality check in all matters teen-related (I mean, can you be more out of touch about us? Please!), but specifically with regard to your total lack of foresight in the area of kissing. Let me tell you what happens when there is no Patron Saint of Kissing, especially for us kissing virgins. I mean, not that I am one or anything—I've kissed plenty of boys in my day. Though, not to say that I overdo it either—I don't want you to think I'm unchaste or something—but anyway. As a result of this deficiency, teenagers, who shall remain nameless to protect their identity, might possibly be praying to saints whose specialization is not kissing, and sources tell me that when this happens, it's like intercessions gone haywire! Girls are getting attacked left and right. Attempts to kiss and then some, if you know what I mean, are made by overzealous boys. And this, I say, is a terrible sin!

Lord knows, it is virtually impossible to get yourself kissed in general without some heavenly intervention, and then before you know it, a little prayer here, a little prayer there, to saints who clearly are not trained in the art of kiss intercession, and suddenly you are in big trouble. I know you might be thinking, "Hmmm. We are not in support of premarital kissing because that has to do with the big S word," but listen, it's not like I'm proposing a Patron Saint of Losing Your Virginity. Kissing is about as innocent as you can get. I mean, when did a little tongue hurt anybody? When? Only when it's misdirected, that's when! Not that *I* would know personally, but this is what I have heard from others.

And finally, this is a matter of teenage purity!

Girl teenage purity especially, because I believe it's the boys who are most responsible for kissing confusion. And isn't that your favorite topic? Protecting a girl's purity? And I, Antonia, being named after the Patron Saint of Teenage Purity herself (well, it was an accident really, the naming thing, since supposedly I was named after Anthony, but my mother didn't do all her homework on the name thing)—I implore you to realize that naming a Patron Saint of the First Kiss and Kissing is essential to prevent haphazard kissing from becoming rampant in Catholic high schools across America, and I am sure Italy, too! It may already be at crisis levels.

Thank you for your attention to this matter.

Blessings,
Antonia Lucia Labella
Labella's Market of Federal Hill
33 Atwells Avenue
Providence, RI USA
saint2b@live.com

P.S. I humbly offer myself as the ideal candidate to not only become the Patron Saint of the First Kiss and Kissing, but the first ever living saint in Catholic history! Come on, you could use a little good PR these days, if you get what I'm saying. Hope to hear from you soon!

I folded up the letter and stuffed it inside one of the air-mail envelopes I kept in my Saint Diary, carefully sealing the flap. This midmonth change of plans required special action, so I decided to ask Gram for a ride to the post office in her Lincoln Town Car. I'd overnight my letter to the Vatican, special delivery, since tomorrow was a Saturday.

Desperate situations required desperate measures.

No thanks to St. Jude, that was for sure.

"Stupid St. Augustine! You and your lecherous ways," I said, jumping up from my bed, a new sense of purpose coursing through my veins. "Antonia of Providence, Patron Saint of the First Kiss," I said, thinking how ironic my new proposal was. I hadn't even gotten myself kissed yet — for-real kissed, at least — and there I was recommending myself as the Patron Saint of Kissing. Ha!

Hidden in the back of the drawer in my vanity was a single tube of lipstick in a deep shade of red. Even though it was against my mother's rules, I was feeling bold and decided to put some on. A Patron Saint of the First Kiss would *obviously* wear lipstick. I found the matching lip liner and carefully drew a thin outline around my mouth, noticing in the mirror how the red color gave my lips a fullness, even a brightness. Maybe girls wore lipstick as a creative way to mark the spot where boys were *supposed* to kiss, directing them away from other, less appropriate first-kiss places.

Like, for example, girls generally didn't apply lipstick in the boob area.

I threw on my uniform with lightning speed, and took

one last look in the mirror, admiring my pouty red lips. I'd shower later, before the guests arrived for the party. It wasn't as if I had anyone to impress today since Andy Rotellini had fallen from grace big-time, TAKING MY HEART WITH HIM.

"Grandma!" I yelled, grabbing the letter. By tomorrow morning someone in Rome would be opening my newest appeal—the most urgent one yet. On a whim, I planted a big red kiss over the seal. Satisfied, I headed out the door to find Gram standing in the hall, purse and keys in hand, as if she'd known I needed her help. "The post office and then on to school," I said.

"Whatever you need, sweetheart," she answered, glancing at the letter, nodding her head. She reached up, wiping the corner of my mouth, a red smear staining her fingers. "That's better."

"Thanks, Gram."

The two of us swept past my mother, standing infuriated and alone before three unfinished mounds of pasta dough. I was too busy to care, praying Gram would make it to the post office in time.

Sainthood was calling me.

19

Maria and I Debrief "The Unthinkable" and She Tells Me Her "Other Ideas"

H e did *what*? *Where*?"

Maria and I were sitting in the school cafeteria at lunch and I was giving her the scoop about The Andy Attack. We were alone at one end of a long Formica-topped table leaning over slices of pizza and Cokes. The buzz of everyone else talking gave us some semblance of privacy.

"In the storeroom, up against the wall," I said. "At first I was all, you know, breathless and excited and everything."

"Well, *yeah*. Who wouldn't be? I remember the first time John was about to kiss me—"

"Can we please focus?"

"Yes. Sorry," she said, wiping away the dreamy look she always got about John. "I'm listening. Undivided."

"So there I am, pinned against the wall, in my *pajamas*, feeling grateful I made the commitment to wear a bra even while sleeping—"

"You *what*?"

"I decided like a month ago that I'd start a twenty-four-hour-a-day bra-wearing campaign in my effort to become more saintly. That part isn't important, though. The main thing is, THANK AGATHA, Patron Saint of All Things Boob-Related, that I was wearing something underneath my tank top so Andy couldn't, you know, *see* or *touch* anything he wasn't supposed to."

"I thought you said saint specializations having to do with boobs were off-limits."

"Only if they have to do with boob enhancement, not boob concealment or boob disorders."

"Really?"

"Yes. Can I get on with my story, please?"

"So you're wearing a bra under your pajamas and Andy has you pinned against the wall . . ."

"And there's this box of something behind me—I think it was instant polenta—digging into the back of my legs, so I'm not exactly comfortable. But at the time, I am trying not to care, of course."

"Absolutely."

"So I can feel his breath against my face, he's so close, and I'm thinking this is it! Andy Rotellini is FINALLY GOING TO KISS ME, so I close my eyes, getting ready for the kiss, even though, you know, it's not at all how I expected our first kiss to happen, at six-thirty in the morning and all, when I'm covered in flour and have a wicked case of bed-head. But anyway, he has one of his hands touching the skin on my arm and my neck, which at first feels really sexy and good and which I *presume* means we are headed somewhere romantic, like, you know, he's going to brush the side of my cheek, like in the movies."

"But . . ."

"But suddenly I realize his hand is not headed anywhere romantic or sweet like my face and neither are his lips! *Suddenly* one hand is sliding the strap of my tank top off my shoulder while the other is moving YOU KNOW WHERE up under my shirt and his mouth is, like, heading across my chest with absolutely no respect for the presence of my bra, if you know what I mean," I said, getting upset all over again. "I can't even say it out loud."

"Wow. That's, um, a bit forward of him."

"And then he's all pressed up against me!"

"Against the wall?"

"Yes! Good thing I shoved him before he reached any of his ultimate destinations."

"You shoved him?"

"Yeah. Hard. Right into the boxed capellini. He knocked it right over."

"Go, Antonia. He so deserved to be shoved. I'm proud of you for standing up to him like that. What a total and shocking disappointment, though."

"My LIPS, Maria! He was supposed to kiss my lips, not my boobs! I mean, who wants her first kiss to be a boob-kiss? I swear to I don't know *what saint*, since I'm through with petitioning them for help in this area, it is seriously impossible for me to get kissed."

"Obviously Andy just wasn't the right guy, Antonia,"

Maria said. "But there will be somebody who *is* right. I promise you. As your best friend in the entire world, I swear it will happen and it will be wonderful when it does."

"I thought it would feel different, Maria. Having a chance with Andy," I said with a sigh.

"I know," she said with sympathy. "This is hugely unfortunate."

"I finally get to the moment I've been waiting for," I continued, picking at the pizza crust, "you know, with Andy standing there looking like he wants me. But he doesn't really want *me*, he only wants the body parts of me." It made me shudder to even think about the whole fiasco. "I obviously didn't get the saint-kissing-request thing right. First, I pray to celibate Jude, who basically ignores me. Then I petition the horniest known saint in history. I should have known better than to pray to a saint who could barely keep his pants on for something as innocent as a kiss. Of course St. Augustine botched it up."

"Hey, lower your voice," Maria whispered. "Your favorite person just sat down two tables away."

"That's all I need right now." I sighed, glancing left. "Veronica learning about my Andy disaster. *And* on the day of the party."

"She's jealous of you, Antonia."

"Jealous of what?"

"More like jealous of *who*," Maria said.

"Michael?"

"Yeah, Michael. He follows you around like an adoring

puppy and Veronica is totally in love with him." She paused, taking a sip from her Coke. "Hey. Do you think this could have been some sort of revenge on Veronica's part? You know, like, she told Andy to do all that? Or told him you *wanted* things to happen like that?"

"Nope. I am confident this was Augustine's fault. Who I am currently on the outs with. I may even have to remove his page from my Saint Diary."

"At least you tried, Antonia."

"I guess. This is also exactly why it was worth the small fortune it cost me to overnight my new proposal for sainthood. I can't even believe I hadn't thought of it before. Since"—I paused for dramatic effect—"a Patron Saint of the First Kiss and Kissing is in dire demand."

"You waited all this time to spill this crucial new information?"

"Well, the post-office excursion with Gram took *forever*, which is why I was late this morning. She drives, like, five miles an hour because she can't really see that well over the dashboard. My original plan was to tell you everything in the parking lot before school."

"I can't believe your mother hasn't taken the keys away yet."

"Once we finally got to the post office I found out it cost almost seventy dollars to send a package overnight to Italy and I only had fifty. I knew it would be expensive, but not *that bad*." Recalling the painful hit to my savings account made me wince. "Gram offered to cover the difference, but of course she couldn't find her wallet."

184

"Because she buried it in the yard with the fig trees last weekend?"

Maria's comment made me laugh for the first time since the beginning of lunch. I took another bite of my pizza—nowhere near as good as my mother's. "So anyway, we detour to the bank, and Gram doesn't have a bank card because she's convinced people will steal her money through the machine, so we have to wait until eight-thirty when the bank opens so she can withdraw money from the teller. Good thing they know her, since she didn't have her ID. Meanwhile, I am practically hyperventilating because I am traumatized, dying to talk to you, but knowing I'm going to be late for school, and having an anxiety attack that we are never going to get this overnight delivery in the mail."

"Well, you *did* send it, and it's over, with Andy, I mean, and now we need to think about you moving on."

"Moving on to what?"

"A new love of your life! The best way to get over one person is to get interested in somebody else," Maria said as if she was an expert on these matters.

"Well . . ." I began, but then stopped. Thoughts of Michael entered my mind—his recent nighttime visits, and Maria's insistence that he respected me, something I may have undervalued in the past. But I pushed them away, reminding myself that we were just friends, and that, besides, he and Veronica had *something* going on between them. Veronica was the last person I needed to cross right now.

"I'm going to go out on a limb here and say that maybe

what happened this morning is a sign, Antonia—which, as you know, is something I almost never do since I'm not at all superstitious and saint-oriented like you are."

"A sign of what?"

"That you are meant to be with somebody else. Maybe St. Augustine even intended that things would go badly with Andy. Because maybe . . ." she said, intrigued, "maybe *Michael* was really who you were supposed to kiss all along. Maybe the entire community of saints has been conspiring to give you both another chance."

"You are being irrational, Maria," I said, with only halfhearted conviction I didn't really feel. Maybe Maria knew my true feelings better than I did. "I'm barely hours away from having two years of dreams dashed to smithereens and you suddenly think Andy was never the love of my life—Michael is?"

"Look who's having trouble taking leaps of faith now." Maria reached over and took a bite out of my crust. "What about Michael? Seriously."

"No. He's involved with Veronica."

"Even if he does have something going on with Veronica—which *he doesn't*, it's all her gossip, no substance—he'd drop her like a calzone just out of the oven if he thought he had a chance with you."

"Stop it, Maria."

"You never know," Maria continued, undeterred by my resistance. "You're the one who's always telling me that."

"I'm through with boys and attempts at getting

kissed—whether it's Michael or anybody else—at least for now."

"Yeah, right. Tonight at the party you'll be complaining to me about how you're dying to find someone new to set your sights on."

"Ohmigosh. The festival of St. Lucia is tonight! And Andy will be there. I can't see him!" I was filled with dread. "It will be too embarrassing!"

"Antonia, if Andy dares show his face tonight, he'll be so sorry he ever laid eyes on you. I'll make sure of it. Trust me."

"Really?"

"Really."

"It's bad enough I need to parade around as a fire hazard in front of the entire neighborhood and half of HA and Bishop Francis," I said, grimacing at the thought of the public display I'd have to face after such a traumatic beginning to my day, not to mention enduring Veronica falling all over Michael in our living room.

"Come on, Antonia. It will be fun. It always is."

"Easy for you to say. You won't be the one with a ring of lit candles on her head."

"At least you get to wear a nice dress."

"Yeah. I can thank Gram for that one." Gram had taken me to the mall yesterday, rescuing me from the hell of my mother's horrible fashion taste. "I'll be the virginal girl in white, despite Andy's attempts to change that about me."

The bell rang, signaling the end of lunch. As we cleared our plates and cups, heading to our next class, I secretly hoped that Maria was right, that tonight would be about moving on, whatever that meant, to a new chapter in the life of Antonia Lucia Labella. A good one. We walked in step with each other, Maria giving my arm an I'm-here-for-you squeeze. With every passing moment my latest letter to the Vatican was closer to its destination and a spark of hope took root in my heart. It helped push away the morning's drama, making me believe that, somehow, good things were still on the horizon. Maybe even kissing.

Maria was right—she knew me too well. I was already back on the topic of kissing. The future Patron Saint of the First Kiss and Kissing had better get her act together. It would be a disgrace if the Vatican called on me and I was in antikissing mode.

If only I knew *who* to kiss.

20

I Try Not to Catch on Fire While I Pass Out Cookies for the Feast of St. Lucia

Stand still, Antonia."

"I am," I told Maria. But I couldn't stop shivering.

Cold December air gusted up the stairs and through the front door as it was opened and closed, opened and closed. The temperature inside must have dropped at least ten degrees since all of Federal Hill began squeezing into our tiny apartment, arriving family by family, to celebrate Saint Lucia's Feast Day.

And it had started to snow, the first snow of the season.

We stood in the doorway of the bathroom, trying to catch a glimpse of the guests as they arrived. Maria was pinning the crown of candles in place on my head. Then she would light them. With matches. "Well, death by fire would certainly fast-track me on the road to sainthood," I said, thinking of all the saints who were burned at the stake—St. Afra, who died of smoke inhalation while her feet were on fire, and Joan of Arc, of course.

"We've already established you are not going to sacrifice your life in order to become a saint, so hold still."

"Amalia!" Aunt Silvia's nasal voice announced her arrival, ringing throughout the house. Her largeness was notable and she was even louder than her wonder triplets, my cousins, who'd arrived earlier. Most likely to get first dibs on all the food.

"*Ciao*, Silvia!" My mother forced a cheery greeting, her voice a mixture of excitement and stress. She wore a plain long black sleeveless dress that fit her beautifully, setting off the olive tone of her skin. Maybe she had a change of heart about dating, I'd thought earlier that evening, when she emerged from her room, glowing and bejeweled in her finest. Mr. D'Agostino had been hovering around her ever since he'd arrived.

"Hello, Vinny, good to see you," I heard my mother say.

Vinny was Francesca's fiancé.

The Romanos were here, the Montaquilas, the Mansolillos, the Sartoros, and countless other families. Mr. Romanelli—the elderly man whose groceries I delivered weekly—had even made it for the celebration. Mr. and Mrs. Rotellini appeared, but there'd been no sign of Andy, thanks be to whatever saint was offering me protection. I remembered Maria's promise and knew I wasn't alone, saints or no saints.

Mrs. Bevalaqua was animated, her voice as clear as a bell, as if her ability to walk again had taken years off. She was a Federal Hill celebrity now. When she passed through the streets people pointed out "The Miracle Lady"—that's what they were calling her—even though for some reason she kept telling everyone that *I* was the real miracle lady. Well, miracle *girl*. Some people even wanted to touch her like they would Mother Teresa, or the Pope.

I saw the McGinnises arrive—Michael's family—with the next-love-of-my-life-according-to-Maria in tow, but he hadn't yet seen me. Veronica was probably throwing herself at him already.

"I bet Michael and Veronica are hanging out right now," I said with a sigh.

"And you care because . . ." Maria moved to where she could survey her work.

"Well, if it wasn't for Veronica . . ." I called to mind what Maria had said at lunch and then again after school, about Michael being my *real* fate, my true love, and all the saints conspiring to bring us together.

"If it wasn't for Veronica, what?"

"I don't know, Maria," I said, and, in truth, I didn't. Not yet, at least. After school I'd finally told Maria about Michael's late-night visits to my window. I usually never held back anything from her, but this . . . this was different. I hadn't been ready to talk about it. But maybe now I was. *Maybe.* "I can't believe I have to do this ridiculous ritual again this year," I said, changing the subject.

"Well, you're always going to be the youngest in the family—at least until Francesca starts having kids with that greasy Vinny guy—and since it's tradition that the youngest girl play the role of St. Lucia, I think you're stuck."

"Thanks for reminding me," I said, dejected at the thought. "If only Veronica was a month younger. Then she'd be St. Lucia tonight, not me. Then I'd get to simply enjoy the party."

"Yeah. Too bad. I'd love to see Veronica's head on fire."

I *had* to stop fidgeting. Maria was beginning to light the candles. All I needed was for hot wax to drip on my head, or worse. She directed me into the bathroom so she could light the rest of the crown. Mom mandated that until I was all lit I had to stay hidden from the guests. That way, when I emerged they could "Ooh!" and "Aah!" at the surprise of it, as if they hadn't seen me lit up like the Fourth of July as St. Lucia for the last eight years running.

"Does it at least comfort you to know that you look seriously hot in that dress? I have to hand it to your gram . . . if she has anything, it's style." Maria stepped back to admire the white V-neck sheath that stopped just above my knees. It had a chiffon overlay with long, transparent sleeves that reached beyond my wrists, making the dress seem ethereal, almost medieval. Though I had the sneaking suspicion it was also the kind of dress that would signal Virgin About to Be Sacrificed in a movie.

Maria's simple black spaghetti-strap dress, her long hair sleek and shiny down her back, made her look sexy and sophisticated on the other hand.

"You are the picture of St. Lucia, my friend!" Maria

gently guided me toward the door. "I'll tell your mother you're ready."

I glanced in the mirror. My head glittered with a burning halo. "Thanks, Maria." I stood as erect as possible. The light in the bathroom was coming entirely from me. I closed my eyes and made a quick petition to St. Lucia while I waited for Maria to return:

St. Lucia, O Patron Saint of Lights, please oh please do not let my head catch on fire tonight in front of the entire neighborhood. It would give Veronica too much satisfaction and me too much humiliation to bear, especially after this morning.

When I opened my eyes Maria was handing me the basket of cookies that I was supposed to give away. It overflowed with fig-filled cookies, wandies, and amaretto biscotti.

"Your mother said to come out. She's quieting the guests."

"Save me, Maria. Please," I groaned.

"It'll be over quick," she reassured me. "I'm going to go sit with John. Good luck!"

With basket in hand, I moved slowly into the hallway, as if I were balancing a stack of books on my head.

"Ah, Antonia," Mr. Sartoro said in a shaky, delighted voice, "you get more *bella* by the day!"

"Um, thanks, Mr. Sartoro," I replied, eyes straight ahead, trying my best to be nice. I offered him a cookie.

Talk only slowed down my parade and I wanted it over as soon as possible.

"Antonia," my mother whispered in my ear from behind, startling me. I almost set fire to the old photographs on the wall.

"What?" I hissed back. "Don't scare me like that!" I already knew she was assessing the length of my dress. She stepped toward me so we were nose-to-nose.

"Antonia Lucia Labella!" I could hear the anger underneath her pretending-to-be-chatting-nicely-to-her-daughter-in-public voice. "Did you shorten that dress?"

"No, I didn't," I said, my eyes wide with innocence. Because it was Gram who had shortened it for me. "Biscotti, Mom?"

"Don't you biscotti me! And don't lie to me either! That dress is immodest! It's above your knees! Everyone is going to think my baby is a *puttana*!" She covered her eyes dramatically. "I know that dress was longer yesterday," she said, pausing, exasperated. "Your *grandmother* did it, didn't she . . . That woman is getting senile, hemming your dress so that you're practically naked."

"Mom, can we finish this later? Now is not exactly the time—"

"O *Madonna*, if it weren't the feast of St. Lucia . . ." she said, shaking her head, trailing off. "Go! Go! Pass the cookies and light the fire so we can all begin eating. At least your arms are covered," she added, mustering a smile before she turned to rejoin the guests.

I continued on, slowly, into the throng of neighbors

packing the kitchen, offering the basket toward whichever hands came into sight, trying to avoid noticing who was watching the spectacle that was me with a ring of fire above my head.

"*Prego*, Antonia Lucia," said a voice that sounded like Mr. Romano's.

"*Prego, bellissima*," said another, a woman's, thanking me as ring-adorned fingers reached for a filled cookie.

Just keep going, I told myself. In about sixty seconds the ordeal would be over.

Michael appeared. I froze.

His stare was intense, his gaze unwavering. His eyes went all the way up and then all the way down, taking me in. It gave me chills. Even as Veronica walked up to whisk Michael away, fawning over him, Michael tore his eyes from me only at the last second, as if he didn't really want to leave but Veronica gave him no choice.

Focus, Antonia. I had to get this ritual over with so I could start getting some answers.

After what felt like forever I entered the living room. Out of the corner of my eye I saw Michael and Veronica sitting on the brown faux-leather couch. I couldn't find Maria and John. Arms reached out to me and I continued to offer the biscotti, filled cookies, and delicate wandies my grandmother had labored over all week. I mustered a smile and noticed how the older people watched me with wistful looks on their faces as I passed.

Suddenly, Veronica was standing in front of me, smirking.

"You're in my way," I said in a low growl, shoving a wandy at her, which hit her in the stomach and immediately crumbled, leaving a trail of pastry bits and powdered sugar down the front of her skirt.

"Look what you did!"

"Sorry," I sang. "Now, out of my way."

"Your mother asked me to finish the ritual," she said, a sneer on her face. She held up a long white candle.

"My mother *what*? I thought Maria was going to do it!"

"You're at my mercy, Antonia, so suck it up," Veronica said, gleeful. "This is over when *I* make it over," she whispered into my ear.

"Fine," I said under my breath, making a beeline for the fireplace, narrowly missing the chandelier overhead, hoping to avoid burning by molten candle wax in the process. Before turning around to face everyone, I composed myself, not wanting to show that I was upset.

I *hated* being at the mercy of Veronica.

Veronica held the unlit candle and key to my freedom in front of her. She smiled as if she had all the time in the world.

"Will you get on with it already," I hissed.

"Thank you, everyone, for being here with us today . . ." Veronica said grandly, pausing as if she were some gracious hostess and not just my dumpy cousin wearing a shirt that screamed, "Look at my boobs! Each one is almost as big as my head."

The living room overflowed with guests. Maria caught

my eye and mouthed, "I'm sorry." I tried to avoid everyone's stares.

". . . to celebrate the festival of Santa Lucia! If everyone would raise their glasses with me."

Veronica plucked a nearby glass of wine from a side table. With the unlit candle in her other hand, she rose up on her tiptoes and set it alight from one of the candles in my crown, as if I were some sort of bizarre liturgical ornament at the front of a church, and then lowered it into the fireplace. A blaze roared to life.

"To St. Lucia!" Veronica shouted. It was so obvious she loved being the center of attention.

"To St. Lucia!" Everyone answered, toasting one another, the room erupting with chatter. Glasses clinked. People hugged and kissed. My mother, grandmother, aunt, and remaining two cousins whisked the food out from the kitchen and onto every available surface. People began to eat the second the trays hit the tables.

"Blow them out, Veronica," I pleaded. That was the last part of the ritual and I was desperate to go to my room and remove the crown.

"Oh, Michael!" she called in a syrupy voice, turning away without a backward glance. "Have you tried the artichokes? They're just *delicious*! Let me get you one."

I stood there helpless, not wanting to move through the crowd for fear of burning everyone I bumped into, wondering to myself whether the motivation behind the Feast of St. Lucia was to torture young girls. Michael looked past Veronica at me, but I avoided his gaze, feeling embarrassed to be made to look like such a child in front of the entire neighborhood, performing this ritual year after year.

Then Maria materialized, candle snuffer in hand, and I thanked St. John, the Patron Saint of Friends and Friendship. I might have been an only child, but I knew how lucky I was to have a best friend who was always, *always* ready to come to my rescue.

21

I Confront an Uninvited Guest in My
Room, Veronica Gets in the Way, and
Catholics the World Over Receive
Shocking News

What are you doing in my room?" I asked, frozen. "Mere surprise" doesn't quite capture what I felt. Mrs. Bevalaqua was about to sing and I didn't want to miss it. I'd been so eager to remove the candelabra on my head, ripping out the bobby pins that were holding it in place and flinging them onto my bed, that I hadn't noticed Michael McGinnis sitting at my vanity. His face was reflected in the mirror. He was smiling. "Shouldn't you be with Veronica or something?"

"Now *why* . . ." he began, swiveling around on the chair, his blue-green eyes wide with amusement, when I noticed that MY SAINT DIARY lay open in his lap.

"Hey!" I interrupted before he could finish. I stormed toward him, hands outstretched. "Give me that! It's private!"

"You really do have a thing for saints, don't you?" His eyebrows were raised, my Saint Diary still open in his lap.

He glanced over at the statue of St. Anthony, and then up at the shelf filled with seven other volumes, and then back at me.

"Um, FYI, you are not really in a position to be asking *me* questions since you are sitting in *my* room, *uninvited*. AND, you are going through my private things, which I want back."

"I'm sorry if you're upset." He sounded relatively sincere. "I was just curious and I didn't really go through any of it, whatever it is," he said, holding the diary out to me.

I took it from his hands and a wave of relief washed over me. My reflection in the mirror behind him reminded me that I still had a crown of candles fastened to my head. Drops of hardened white wax stood out against my hair.

Before I could say "Hey, what do you think you're doing," Michael stood up and was reaching toward my face, causing my stomach to erupt immediately with butterflies, at which point I realized that for the SECOND TIME in one day a boy was about to touch me. At six this morning I'd been so TOTALLY UNTOUCHED and now I was practically DEVIRGINIZED. Though why I had to be wearing a crown of candles and wax in my hair when there was a BOY in my room close enough to touch was beyond me. Even if the boy was only Michael. And even if, as it turned out, he wasn't about to really touch me.

The crown tugged at my curls as he tried to lift it.

"This is on here good, isn't it?" He wore a look of concentration.

"Thanks, but I can handle this," I said, ducking from

his hands, pulling the red vanity chair that suddenly seemed too childish for a high school girl over to the mirror. I sat down and plucked at the remaining bobby pins. I was too embarrassed to pick out the drops of wax so I pretended they weren't there. In the mirror I could see Michael sitting on the edge of my bed, watching me.

There was a BOY sitting ON MY BED.

"You still haven't answered why you're not with Veronica," I said, making conversation. My eyes didn't leave his reflection in the mirror, even as I continued to work at removing my headgear.

"Do you really need me to answer that?"

I didn't respond right away. I was busy, gently lifting the crown off my head, noting that I had a bad case of crown-head: a dent the shape of a circle was branded into my hair. Great.

"Yes, please," I said, spinning around so Michael and I were sitting almost knee-to-knee.

Mrs. Bevalaqua's voice soared from the living room.

"Oh, no, I need to go," I said. "We need to go, I mean. We can't miss Mrs. Bevalaqua's singing . . ." My voice trailed off. Without a word Michael leaned forward, his elbows resting on his knees, his face inches from mine. The sounds of "O mio babbino caro" drifted down the hall. It felt as if we were in a movie. I was transfixed. Unable to move.

My lips parted.

So did his.

I closed my eyes.

"Antonia!" An angry voice disrupted our moment. I sprang up from the chair, bumping into Michael in the process. The last person in the world I wanted to see right then, maybe aside from my mother, burst into my room.

"Hi, Veronica," Michael said as if this were not the most awkward situation we could possibly conjure up.

"Sorry to intrude on you," Veronica said in a voice that was anything but sorry.

"You weren't interrupting anything," I said quickly.

"Yeah, right," she said to me. I was already racing toward the door even though Michael was still sitting on my bed. To Michael she turned and said, "We need to talk."

"I'm sure you do . . . I'll just give you some privacy," I said, shutting the door to my room behind me like an idiot, feeling a painful stab of jealousy. There was still a boy in my room but he was WITH ANOTHER GIRL. Even worse: he was with my cousin! I felt torn. See Mrs. Bevalaqua or eavesdrop on Veronica and Michael? I decided to eavesdrop.

"What, Veronica?" I heard Michael say. He sounded annoyed.

"Why is your ear pressed up against your door, Antonia?" Maria was heading toward me, looking confused. John trailed behind her.

"Shhhh." I held my finger up to my lips. "Veronica and Michael are in my room having a talk," I whispered.

"Why in the world would you let them have a talk in your bedroom? Couldn't they find somewhere else?" Maria sounded shocked.

"I'm trying to listen," I said. Maria mouthed "Sorry" and joined me, her ear to the door now, too. She motioned to John that he should leave us.

"We should go," Michael pleaded. He obviously wanted out.

"What exactly is going on between you and Antonia?"

I felt eager to know Michael's answer to this particular question. It was easier to listen to Michael talk about his feelings for me when I was on the other side of a closed door.

"Nothing," Michael said. "There's never been anything between Antonia and me. It was over before it even began," he added.

My heart sank. The butterflies died.

"Really?" Veronica asked, sounding hopeful.

"Really," he confirmed.

Was Michael playing both of us? Maria looked at me with sympathy.

"Can we finish this conversation later?" Michael asked.

"Look at me, Michael," Veronica was saying. *"Please."*

"Listen, Veronica: I am not, nor will I ever, go out with . . ."

The rest of Michael's sentence was lost. Wailing erupted from the living room. Everything was thrown into chaos. People were shouting, crying, talking loudly to one another. My bedroom door was thrown open and Maria and I were face-to-face with Veronica (who looked livid) and Michael (who seemed upset by the discovery that we'd been listening).

This was not the time for explanations or apologies. Without a word Maria and I raced down the hall to the kitchen. The radio was blaring and through the foyer I could see everyone gathered together, glued to the television in the corner of the living room. Tears rolled down people's faces. Maria and I pushed our way through the crowd.

"What's going on?" I shouted.

"Antonia," my grandmother said when she saw me, enfolding me in a hug. I felt her soft body, her ample chest, squeezing me tightly, making me scared that something terrible had happened.

"Grandma, *what*," I whispered. "Tell me."

"The Pope has died," she whispered back. "Pope Gregory XVII is dead."

22

We Eagerly Await Our New Holy Father

W e are live from St. Peter's Square at the Vatican," the reporter announced. "It is rumored that any moment now the cardinals will be holding the second of their two morning votes. Yesterday we saw only black smoke rising from the chimney of the Sistine Chapel, signaling to the world that it would have to wait at least another day before a new pontiff is named."

One week later, Friday, December 16, the second day of the Vatican conclave was already under way. Cardinals from every corner of the globe had gathered to elect the new leader of the Catholic Church. We'd watched television almost nonstop. Pope Gregory XVII's funeral was held Tuesday in a worldwide day of mourning. Then, with the Christmas holidays upon us, the cardinals shortened the waiting period before conclave to three days following the funeral. Three, after all, is an auspicious number if you are Catholic.

Two fates hung in the balance, as far as I was concerned—one of them *mine*.

Mom and Gram leaned forward on the couch, their eyes glued to The Chimney Channel. The networks had set up a special twenty-four-hour-a-day broadcast of the Sistine Chapel chimney for those who couldn't bear to tear themselves away from the all-important smokestack. Veronica, Concetta, and Francesca sat together in a heap on the opposite side of the living room, alternately yapping and shoving pizzelle cookies in their mouths. Trays of food covered every available surface—you'd think we were having another party. Aunt Silvia and Uncle Alfredo were in the kitchen, making cups of espresso. It could be another long day and night. We had no way of knowing.

Meanwhile, I prayed to St. Peter, the Patron Saint of the Papacy and Popes, that the next vote would be the deciding one. I was desperate to know if the College of Cardinals would play it safe and elect another conservative—someone who would offer only more of the same old tired ways and old tired doctrine—or if they would venture out on a limb and choose someone more in touch with the ways of the world today, someone who might be more amenable to, say, naming the first ever living saint in Catholic history. Besides, if the cardinals didn't make a decision soon, the HA–Bishop Francis Winter Formal scheduled for Tuesday night, the first night of Christmas break, would be canceled. All my clandestine plans for finally making it to my first dance would be shattered, just like my love for Andy that tragic morning that now seemed so long ago.

O St. Peter, Patron Saint of the Papacy and Popes, it is imperative that the cardinals get their butts in gear and elect a new pontiff, ideally one who will be so organized that he will assure that not a single letter is lost, not even one perhaps sent the day His Former Holiness, GXVII, died, since it is surely a sin to let even one plea to the Vatican fall through the cracks, especially one that proposes something of such dire importance to young people the world over, that is, a Patron Saint of First Kisses and Kissing. Furthermore, Catholics still reeling from the shock of GXVII's death, especially those who have important plans tonight, cannot bear to wait any longer to know what direction our new Holy Father will take us, ideally in a progressive one, but any direction will be welcomed at the moment. Please let the next signal be white smoke and bells ringing! Please! Thank you, St. Peter, for your intercession in this matter.

I'd practically been under house arrest since last Friday night, except for Wednesday, the only day between the funeral and the conclave when school was in session and we'd opened the market for shortened hours. No one had left the house since the conclave began. The market would remain closed until a new Pope was named. Aside from a few visits from Maria, I'd been trapped with family. There had been no sign of Michael, not even at my window. This was really starting to bother me, especially after what I overhead him say to Veronica in my bedroom. The only upside was that I hadn't had to see Andy.

"As you can see, everyone is eagerly awaiting the fourth vote since yesterday's conclave began," the reporter continued, looking chilled even though she was bundled up in a long wool coat, gloves, and a scarf. She shivered, glancing behind her at the chimney. "Still no sign, but it should be any minute now. The crowds are very excited. You can feel the anticipation."

"*Madonna*, I am so nervous!" my mother cried out, cutting another slice of Italian sweet bread.

"Why, Amalia? What's happening?" Gram asked, a confused look darkening her face. Since the night of the festival, Gram had taken a turn for the worse in the memory department.

"The Pope, Ma," my mother responded, annoyed. "We're waiting to see who the new Holy Father is."

"Oh, how nice!" Gram smiled, munching on a small block of torrone. "I love the Pope!"

"Any news yet?" Aunt Silvia entered the living room holding a tray of tiny steaming cups of espresso. She lumbered over to the coffee table, her wide backside blocking my view of the television.

"Thank you, Silvia," my mother said, taking one of the small white cups and saucers, and sipping the dark, foamy liquid. There was an unspoken truce between them out of respect for this difficult time. My mother squished over toward Gram, making room on the couch for Aunt Silvia. No small feat. "Here," my mother said, patting the space. "Have a seat."

Veronica, Concetta, and Francesca began squealing.

"There he is again!" exclaimed Concetta.

"Ooooh! He's so gorgeous," Francesca said, practically drooling onto our old braided rug. My cousins had been periodically freaking out over a striking, very young, very hot guy with long, golden hair who kept walking between the Sistine Chapel and St. Peter's Basilica as the throng of reporters watched eagerly outside the gates. He was dressed in black flowing robes and the cameras followed him, as if somehow smoke signals were going to spring from the top of his head.

"Frankie! Watch your mouth," Aunt Silvia said, ashamed. "You are an engaged woman."

"Yeah, Ma, I know," she answered back, her eyes never leaving the screen.

Just then the camera panned to the chimney. The crowd outside the Sistine Chapel stirred in excitement.

"*Madonna!* Maybe this is it!"

Gram, Aunt Silvia, and my mother huddled together, hands clasped. I leaned forward, eager to know the outcome of this crucial moment. Meanwhile, Veronica, Concetta, and Francesca continued on about the blond boy's eyes, nose, high cheekbones, and how the robes unfortunately hid his hot body.

And we waited.

And waited.

I said a quick prayer to St. Expeditus, the Patron Saint Against Procrastination, asking that the cardinals speed up the process, get it over with already, put us all out of the misery of waiting, of having life on hold until this decision was made.

"Smoke is beginning to pour from the chimney," the reporter said.

Everyone held their breath . . .

"It's white! We have a new Pope!"

Cheers erupted in St. Peter's Square and in our living room. We were all jumping up, hugging, kissing. Espresso cups were overturned but nobody cared. The phone rang and rang again. Uncle Alfredo emerged from the kitchen, a stain of sauce down the side of his mouth, and my aunt almost knocked him over between her excitement and hefty girth.

"Why is everybody so excited, Antonia?" Gram leaned over and asked me, her brow furrowed.

"Because we have a new Pope," I whispered, giving her a big hug and kissing her on both cheeks.

"Oh, how wonderful," she exclaimed, a smile on her face. "I hope he's a good-looking one."

"Gram!" I said, laughing, thinking that the only way he'd even be remotely good-looking was if the cardinals did something drastic and elected someone under the age of seventy. Then again, maybe a seventy-year-old man would be more Gram's style. I quietly thanked St. Peter and St. Expeditus for their quick response, and breathed a sigh of relief that now the dance on Tuesday wouldn't be canceled.

"Shh, shhh, shhhhhhhh!" My mother hushed everyone.

"Any moment now the new pontiff will emerge from

the balcony of St. Peter's Basilica to address the world for the first time," the reporter explained as the millions packing the square surged forward in excitement. "People are eager to see who the cardinals have chosen and to hear the first words of their new Holy Father. Will he be Italian? Have the cardinals entrusted this holy office to one of the two young favorites—Cardinal Gutierrez from Brazil and Cardinal Esposito from Naples—or have they chosen conservatively yet again, electing someone similar to Gregory XVII, who was already seventy-one when he became Pope fifteen years ago?"

"Oooooh, there he is again!" Concetta shrieked, pointing to the television, where, just behind the reporter, we caught another glimpse of the mysterious hottie. I found it hard to believe that my three cousins were oblivious to the fact that we were about to receive the news we'd all been waiting for because they were focused on some random Vatican aide.

I moved out from behind Aunt Silvia so I'd have a clear view of the television.

The doors to the balcony overlooking St. Peter's Square opened . . .

. . . and a man wearing the standard issue papal hat strode through.

Gasps were uttered all around.

It was Cardinal Esposito. They chose the cardinal from Naples!

"Introducing Pope Gregory Paul IV," said the reporter dramatically.

They did it, I thought. They actually did it. They chose a young, progressive pope!

As the cheering all around me resumed, I made a quick petition to St. Gabriel, praying that even on the days when popes went to their deaths, the mail arrived safely, securely, and was forwarded promptly into the right hands, i.e., those of the new Holy Father. I was sure now more than ever that if anyone would gamble on the first living saint in Catholic history, it would be Cardinal Esposito.

Excuse me: Pope Gregory Paul IV!

PART 3:

The Patron Saint of First Kisses
and Kissing

To: askthevatican@vatican.va

From: Antonia Lucia Labella [STMP: saint2b@live.com]

Subject: URGENT: Overnighted Letter Proposal

Sent: December 16, 10:45 a.m.

To Whom It May Concern (ideally the newly elected Pope if he's available):

First I'd like to offer up my heartfelt CONGRATULA-TIONS about the election of Cardinal Esposito (well, Pope Gregory Paul IV) as our next Holy Father. What fantastic fortune for Catholics the world over, especially young ones like me! Of course, this is *not* to say that we do not mourn and wail for the death of the old pontiff, who will be remembered fondly by all, especially since you (I'm speaking specifically to Pope GPIV here) immediately put him on the road to sainthood the day of his funeral. Now, this act gives me pause, and, if I may point out, this is the THIRD time in recent history that the waiting period for someone's elevation to sainthood has been waived. I mean, we've gone from a fifty-year waiting period to a five-year one to zero in barely the blink of an eye!

Which brings me to the second reason for this e-mail. Pope Gregory Paul IV's new reign is cause for great cele-bration, and what better way to rejoice than by taking the sainthood process *one teeny step further*? I mean, every-body loves a saint. What's there not to love? We can talk to them, ask them for things, they give us comfort. We can pick and choose our favorites and there is oh-so-much variety. But so far, *they have all been dead!* Let me assure you, I am not complaining since I still talk to them all the time and it doesn't bother me in the least that they have gone on to the big palace in the sky like my dad. But I have a fantastic idea for how GPIV can really show the world that he's a Pope *in the know*, a pontiff *on the cutting edge*, a Holy Father *ready to shepherd Catholics into the 21st century!*

GPIV should name the first living saint in Catholic history! It would really make a statement, I am confident.

This brings me to the third reason for this e-mail. I overnighted a *deeply important* letter to the Vatican Committee on Sainthood and to the attention of our dearly departed pontiff on the day of his tragic death. Amid all the uproar of the shock, the grieving, the funeral planning, I was wondering—did anybody sign for it? I mean, I should have opted for the confirmation of receipt when I sent it in the first place, but it was already expensive enough and I just didn't have the extra cash and Gram was already spotting me a few. I know you guys are busy and all, having just held the conclave (by the way, do you get to eat during that, or do they make you fast as an incentive to get it over with quicker?) and with preparing to celebrate our new Holy Father, but could somebody get back to me about whether or not you received my letter? I mean, I don't want to be a bother or anything, it's just that this letter was *super important* and I would feel so much better knowing that it arrived.

Without going into detail, I'll just say it's an urgent matter of teenage-girl purity.

Thanks so much for your help, and again, my condolences and congratulations.

Blessings,
Antonia Lucia Labella
Labella's Market of Federal Hill
33 Atwells Avenue
Providence, RI USA
saint2b@live.com

P.S. You can just respond with a quick e-mail to my inquiry. Really. No fancy letters with the Vatican seal or anything necessary. Just confirmation that the letter is in someone's holy hands!

• • •

To: askthevatican@vatican.va

From: Antonia Lucia Labella [STMP: saint2b@live.com]

Subject: URGENT: Patron Saint of the First Kiss and Kissing

Sent: December 17, 3 p.m.

Attachment: *kissingletter.doc*

To Whom It May Concern (ideally the newly elected Pope if he's available):

Now that you've had some time to digest the wonderful news about our new pontiff (and a special hello to you, GPIV, if you are reading this ☺), I wanted to take this opportunity to introduce myself more formally. My name is Antonia Lucia Labella, I am fifteen years old (almost sixteen!), I live in Federal Hill, the proud Italian community of Providence, RI, and I am a big fan of the Vatican! I'd like to direct your attention, if you have not already done so— I don't know if you all switch jobs immediately with the new Pope and all, you know, like here in the U.S., when there's a new president, I mean, they just totally clear out the old administration to make room for the new—to my file kept in the Office of the Vatican Committee on Sainthood. If someone could just please take a second and make note of it, I'd really appreciate it.

And speaking of my file, if when you pull it out you happen to notice at the very top there is a letter proposing a Patron Saint of the First Kiss and Kissing, could you (a) read the proposal in its entirety and consider it care-

218

fully and (b) shoot me a quick e-mail letting me know it arrived? I'd really appreciate it.

Thanks again for your time.

Blessings,

Antonia Lucia Labella

Labella's Market of Federal Hill

33 Atwells Avenue

Providence, RI USA

saint2b@live.com

• • •

To: askthevatican@vatican.va

From: Antonia Lucia Labella [STMP: saint2b@live.com]

Subject: URGENT: Patron Saint of the First Kiss and Kissing

Sent: December 19, 9:35 p.m.

Attachment: *antoniatoastingnewpope.jpg*

To Whom It May Concern (ideally the newly elected Pope if he's available):

It's me again. You know, Antonia Lucia Labella from Providence—the girl with the big file of letters proposing a wide variety of strangely overlooked saintly specializations that goes back almost nine years. If it hasn't caught your eye already, let me draw your attention to my latest campaign, that of the DESPERATE need for a Patron Saint for the First Kiss and Kissing, which, I assure you, is not only ideal for replacing the now fallen from grace St.

Valentine (I mean, no one can fault you for defrocking him and everything, since who needs a saint who *never even existed*, and speaking of which, let me take this moment to assure you that I, on the other hand, am very, *very* existent), but a Patron Saint of the First Kiss and Kissing would appeal to young people everywhere *and* celebrate the innocent side of love! And you guys love innocence over there, so I urge you to PLEASE READ MY LETTER if you have not already, and then send me a brief, even one-word (just a YES would do) confirmation that you received it.

Thanks!

Blessings,
Antonia Lucia Labella
Labella's Market of Federal Hill
33 Atwells Avenue
Providence, RI USA
saint2b@live.com

P.S. I attached a new photo for my file! It's a picture of me toasting our new Holy Father as my family celebrates his wonderful first words to the world as Pope. And don't worry, that *is* red wine in my glass, but I'm only allowed to drink it at Sunday meals and on special occasions, like the election of a new pontiff. Though, not that it really matters, since you don't even have a drinking age in Italy, do you?

• • •

To: askthevatican@vatican.va

From: Antonia Lucia Labella [STMP: saint2b@live.com]

Subject: URGENT: Testing

Sent: December 20, 2:06 p.m.

Hello?

This is a TEST e-mail. Is anybody there? Are you receiving my e-mails? If so, can you respond with a quick YES? It will only take a second, and let me tell you, that second would add YEARS to my future right now if you know what I mean.

Thanks!

Antonia Lucia Labella

Labella's Market of Federal Hill

33 Atwells Avenue

Providence, RI USA

saint2b@live.com

23

MARIA AND I MAKE OURSELVES LOOK
IRRESISTIBLE, AND SHE TRIES TO CONVINCE ME
OF WHAT MY HEART SHOULD ALREADY KNOW

I thought this day would never come.

It was Tuesday evening, the night of the Winter Formal and the beginning of holiday break. Maria and I stood next to each other, putting on makeup in her parents' bathroom, sharing the mirror.

The television blared in the background. "People are camped throughout St. Peter's Square, awaiting yet another audience with the new pontiff. He has already shocked Catholics all over the world with his progressive vision. There's been talk of women priests, gay marriage, and lifting the ban on birth control. Pope Gregory Paul IV has indicated that these issues and others are up for discussion. This has caused many Catholics to rejoice, but others are furious . . ."

My heart was racing. I was excited. I was anxious. Despite the urgent e-mails I'd sent to the Vatican, I'd heard nothing in response to my latest proposal. But then, I figured I should give the Holy Father a few days to adjust and I had other things on my mind, too. I was headed to my first dance. I had to thank St. Emiliana, the Patron Saint of Single Laywomen, and St. Theobald, the Patron Saint of Single Men, that, unless you had a boyfriend or a girlfriend, most people went stag.

"You girls have a nice rest tonight," my mother said as we were walking out the door earlier. Maria had come to pick me up. I was borrowing one of her dresses so my overnight bag wouldn't look suspicious. "And give your mother my thanks for hosting Antonia and making dinner. I need a break this evening after all this hoopla at the Vatican, *Madonna.*"

"Of course," Maria answered, smiling. "I'll tell her as soon as we walk in the door."

"And here," my mother added, handing Maria a stack of tabloid newspapers in Italian. "Give these to your mother."

"Thanks, Mrs. Labella. She'll be thrilled," Maria said, taking them.

"Bye, Ma," I said, giving her a peck on the cheek, dying to be off to Maria's. "Have a nice night with Gram. We'd better go. We don't want to be late for dinner." I grabbed Maria's arm and we headed toward the door.

"Antonia! Maria!"

I rolled my eyes at my friend and nodded to the holy water next to the door. Dipping our fingers, we crossed ourselves and ran down the stairs, yelling "Bye!" as we went.

"Jesus thanks you," my mother called. Her voice echoed down the stairwell as we reached the bottom, jumped in Maria's car, and sped off to her house.

"What do you think of all this upheaval, Bill?" The discussion from the television talking heads returned me to the task at hand: making myself look fantastic for the dance. "Well, there's been speculation that Gregory Paul IV might even consider letting the clergy marry," said the man named Bill.

"Here, try this lipstick," Maria said, handing me a black tube with a thick band of gold around the middle. "It's your favorite shade of red."

"Pope Gregory Paul IV is wasting no time making a splash in his new reign, that's certain," another voice continued. "But letting the clergy marry? I don't know that the Catholic hierarchy is ready to make that drastic a move."

I took the cap off the lipstick, and inspected the deep color.

"Ooooh," I exclaimed. "It's the same one Gram gave me. I love it. It's perfect!"

"Perfect for kissing, don't you think? Hmmm?" Maria proposed.

"I'm through worrying about that ambition. No more petitioning the saints about kissing, since they either ignore you or mess things up," I said, staring at the lipstick in my hand, thinking how ironic it was to make such a proclamation while at the same time pestering the Vatican about a

Patron Saint of the First Kiss and Kissing. "Case in point: The Andy Attack."

"Antonia." Maria opened her mouth wide as she applied mascara to her already long eyelashes. "The thing with Andy, I admit, was unexpected. I thought he liked you."

"But he didn't," I said, sighing. "Which is why I'm washing away all thoughts of boys and kissing from my mind. It gets too complicated."

"You can't go around proposing that kind of a saint and then be *anti*kissing! It just doesn't add up," Maria said, her voice reproachful. She put down the mascara to give me her full attention. "And second . . . you're ridding yourself of *all* thoughts of boys?" Maria was skeptical.

"Every last one."

"Even thoughts about Michael?" Maria let his name hang in the air. I looked in the mirror. Maria was right. This lipstick was the perfect color.

"Yes, even thoughts of Michael," I said, heading into Maria's bedroom, where dresses, stockings, and other related formal wear were strewn everywhere. She followed me and sat down on the bed. "Especially after overhearing that conversation between Michael and Veronica."

"So you *do* care," Maria said, nodding her head like she'd known all along. "Antonia, did it occur to you that he just said those things to get Veronica off his back? Or even as a favor to *you*? After all, he knows that she treats you like dirt."

"I heard what he said, Maria, and it was not favorable and I am just going to forget about it." Talk of Michael was making my stomach churn. "I don't want any more run-ins with Veronica. And anyway, they were all over each other at the St. Lucia party. You saw, too."

"Yeah. She was all over *him* and not vice versa. I noticed *that* part."

"Same difference."

"Regardless of what you think, *I* am confident that his eyes are only for you. Are you blind or what?"

"He has eyes for everybody."

"Well, whatever. He has special eyes for you, then. And you have to admit, they are *very* nice eyes. Not as nice as John's, but still."

At the mention of John, I leaped at the opportunity to change the subject.

"Speaking of John—"

"Nope. Last time I checked, we were talking about Michael. Don't even try to get out of this conversation. Come on. Let's be honest. I'm your best friend. And you like him, right?" She pulled me up off the bed so we were face-to-face. "I know you, Antonia. I've known you for ten whole years and there is something between you guys that I haven't seen between you and anybody else. Isn't that enough?"

Instead of answering, I walked over to the closet where my dress was hanging, the dress that I was going to wear to my first formal dance. It was beautiful, I thought, running my hand across the crimson taffeta—beautiful and old-fashioned. Strapless. Practically an antique and more of a ball gown than a semiformal, but I didn't care. Maria had pulled it from storage in their attic. Her grandmother had worn it years ago.

"It's perfect for you, isn't it," Maria said, stopping to admire the dress with me. "The way the skirt gathers in those little tufts, and the row of buttons in the back. And the color. I knew you'd love it."

"I do," I said, putting my arm around her. "Thank you for finding it."

"Just part of the best-friend job duties," she said.

"To be totally honest, Maria, there may be some kind of interesting vibe going on between Michael and me," I rambled before I lost the courage. "I might like him a teeny bit. But it's so weird, the whole Veronica-Michael thing, and I've spent two years convincing myself that I was in love with Andy Rotellini."

Maria had a satisfied smirk on her face. We continued to stare at each other in the mirror. "I *knew* you had a thing for him. Maybe you really were supposed to end up with Michael two summers ago and Andy was, I don't know, this unfortunate detour or distraction. And all this time you've been petitioning the saints for help with Andy when really *they* knew what was best for you, but you were so persistent about him that they finally realized you needed a major wake-up call—shock to the system or something. And now that this has all been made clear, you can finally end up with the guy who really knows you and respects you. And maybe even *is in love with you*: Michael."

"Maria," I said, getting goose bumps, "I think you might be going a bit overboard . . ."

"Antonia," she said, still serious, "you know how there are these guys who can't settle on one girl. But it's not so much that they want to be with a bunch of different girls and more that they can't find the *right* girl. And once they do find the right one they're done with all other members of the female species." She turned to look me in the eye. "*You* are *that* girl for Michael. You are the girl who converts his wild ways. All other girls pale in comparison to you. And I think it's romantic," she added, sighing. "You should start praying to one of those saints you love so much for, I don't know, some grace for the evening ahead of us. Isn't Teresa the Patron Saint of Grace?"

"Yes," I said, impressed by Maria's memory. Maybe my saint knowledge was rubbing off on her. "But no way," I continued, "am I going to ask another saint for help with a boy after what I've been through."

"Well, there must be *somebody* you'd trust to help," she said, thinking, tapping her index finger against her chin. "Actually . . . you know what? *I* can think of one! St. Anthony of Padua, your favorite. St. Anthony, if you are listening, please help Antonia find her senses about how Michael really feels about her and how she feels about him. *There.*"

"Maria, I think you're getting ahead of yourself. Though that's really sweet of you to pray to St. Anthony on my behalf, especially since you're not the praying type and all," I said, touched by the gesture. "But just because I admitted a little *like* for Michael doesn't mean I'm going to run out and kiss him or something."

"Why not, Antonia?" Maria interrupted, passionate. "Michael is *not* Andy. And, I mean, are you never going to let anybody touch you? It's going to happen sometime. Why not kiss him tonight? Why *not* Michael?"

"It's just—"

"Antonia, come on."

"You really think Michael's the perfect boy for me?"

"Not as perfect as that dress you're about to put on," she said, cracking a grin. "I don't know about you, but I'm definitely not going to this dance in just stockings and a bra."

"Bet that would make John happy," I said, laughing.

When we were finally dressed and zipped and buttoned and ready to go, Maria and I stood in front of the long mirror in her room, admiring the results of our hard work. Me in my old-fashioned red gown and Maria in her sophisticated black cocktail dress.

"I'm glad I convinced you to wear your hair down," Maria said.

"You don't look so bad yourself."

"Relax, Antonia. Tonight is going to be all about fun . . . and speaking of tonight, it's time to be off for our magical winter evening."

"A magical evening in the HA gym?"

"Use your imagination," she said, pushing her head against mine. We smiled together in the mirror, as if someone was about to take our picture or we were posing in a photo booth. "Besides, *you* are the one who sees miracles everywhere, aren't you? Just close your eyes when we get there and imagine it really *is* a glamorous ball, celebrating your beautification!"

"Beatification," I said, correcting her, even though silently I agreed with her slight change. "And you think *I* get carried away."

"How about letting Michael carry you away."

"Quit it!" I said, but I was laughing.

A car honked outside.

"That's John," Maria said, excitement in her voice.

"Maria? Antonia?" Mrs. Romano was yelling, having no idea she was playing into a major deception being perpetrated on my mother. "Your ride is here."

"Coming!" Maria called out.

We took one last look at ourselves and then we were darting down the stairs, yelling goodbye to Maria's mother, and out the door. Butterflies were flitting this way and that, making my entire body feel tingly.

And for the first time in as long as I could remember, I asked nothing from any saint about the evening ahead.

24

MY HEART GOES PITTER-PATTER AND I
FINALLY UNDERSTAND WHAT IT MEANS TO GET
WEAK IN THE KNEES

D o you want to dance?" an unidentified boy asked,
nervous. He looked young, maybe a freshman. His
jacket and pants were baggy, as if his mother bought them
several sizes too big because he'd grow into them eventually. He pushed his thick, black-rimmed glasses up with his
index finger, waiting for my response. We were the same
height.

Why wasn't Maria glued to my side instead of John's?
Then she could rescue me from this uncomfortable situation. Why hadn't Maria prepared me for how to handle
random boys asking me to dance?

"Maybe later," I said finally, feeling bad about rejecting
him. But my greater fear of three minutes of awkward slow
dancing trumped the guilt.

I crossed the packed, darkened HA gym, weaving my
way between dancing couples to the sea of round tables in
the back, each with a centerpiece of white flowers. Hun-

dreds of tiny, sparkling snowflakes hovered above us, as if a snowfall had frozen in the sky. It was actually pretty. But it wasn't enough to make me forget that I was in the Holy Angels gym and not some magical winter wonderland.

My borrowed heels click-clacked even over the music and forced my hips to sway left and right in a way I wasn't used to. My dress swished with a satisfying rustle, and for once I felt beautiful. I reminded myself to keep my shoulders back and my chin up to accentuate the neckline—it was strapless—like Maria had instructed me earlier.

"Hey, Antonia," I heard someone call out, and I glanced around for the source.

"Antonia!" Lila and Hilary yelled in unison from a table where two Bishop Francis boys sat between them like a divider—not the hockey players I'd seen them with last month, but guys I knew by sight from watching them play baseball with Andy. The reminder of Andy made me feel queasy—I hadn't seen him yet and I hoped we wouldn't cross paths.

"Hi, guys," I said, plopping myself into the chair next to Lila, who immediately turned to me and said, "Soooo . . ." in a leading voice that implied I should somehow know what bit of gossip she expected was in my possession.

"Soooo what?" I asked, confused.

"Is Andy here?" she whispered, giggling.

"I honestly don't know and hope he stays home tonight," I said. Lila looked dismayed, so I filled her in— not on what happened in the storeroom, but with enough detail to explain why I would not be dancing even once with Andy Rotellini.

"You should go back to your guy, Lila," I said once I'd finished the story, nodding to the cute blond next to her. I could hear Hilary talking on about the finer points of the penalty kick to her guy, who seemed genuinely intrigued by a girl absorbed by sports talk.

"Let me introduce you," Lila offered.

I stopped her before she caught his attention, and whispered, "I'd rather meet him another night." When she scrunched her face in confusion I added, "I'm not exactly in the mood to meet one of Andy's baseball buddies."

This she understood.

"I'll be okay," I reassured her. "I'm just going to sit here awhile if you don't mind." And be the fifth wheel, I thought.

"Of course not," she said, eventually turning back to flirt with the blond boy.

Maria was the only person I'd told the full details about the storeroom debacle with Andy, but as I sat there people-watching my classmates—some in beautiful dresses, some in tiny slips that looked like lingerie they could have bought at Victoria's Secret, it was hard not to notice how many of the Bishop Francis guys were friends with Andy. I wondered what he might have blabbed. I consoled myself that *I'd* rejected *him*, which was not the kind of thing a guy wanted to boast about.

But I still felt uneasy.

I craned my neck to see where I'd left Maria and John thirty minutes ago. They hadn't moved an inch and were making out as if the world might end tomorrow.

Wow. They were really going at it. I couldn't stop myself from staring. Was *that* what kissing was supposed to be? It almost looked, I don't know, *violent*. Like what if they choked on each other's tongues? All I knew was that this was *not* what I wanted out of kissing. At least I didn't think so. It looked so *intense*. But, then again, maybe that's exactly what I'd want if I was with a guy I both liked and was kissing (and who was kissing me back). I was surprised that one of the teacher chaperones hadn't noticed or separated them yet.

They did this at Catholic schools. Separated kissing couples. "Let the Holy Ghost be between you." That's what they said. Seriously. Sometimes it was the nuns from HA. Sometimes the brothers from Bishop Francis. Regardless, PDA (Public Display of Affection) was not permitted. At least not officially.

I was still searching the crowd to see who else was there when my eyes found Andy. My stomach lurched. The former love of my life had already found a nice HA junior to occupy his tongue and hands. The thought of how much time I'd wasted on this boy who really did have girls lining up to be with him made me feel foolish.

"Hey, love. You made it," said a welcome voice behind me, the one I'd been hoping to hear since the second we'd arrived. Suddenly two hands were on my shoulders.

"Hi, Michael," I said, forcing myself to sound casual, turning to look up at him. He was grinning, possibly because he was in the perfect position to stare down—or, rather, *at*—my nonexistent cleavage.

"You wore your hair down," he said, picking up one of my curls, playing with it. I had to remind myself to breathe. "You never wear your hair down."

That Michael was standing over me had started to make me feel vulnerable, so I popped up from my chair and turned so we could face each other. But he was standing so close that the skirt of my gown crushed up against him, and the table behind me prevented me from taking a step back. Michael made no indication that he was about to put any more distance between us.

"Hi," I greeted him again, since nothing else came to mind. "Um, do you mind?" I gestured that I needed some space.

"But I like it here," he said, smiling.

"Michael, *please*."

He complied, but as if I'd requested he find a better vantage point from which to take in all of me now, from the tiny silver heels that peeked out from under my dress to the way Maria had styled my hair to spill everywhere. I was not so unnerved that I failed to notice that Michael was far from his usual disheveled state. I'd never seen him dressed up and he looked good, hot even. But then, the way his long messy waves fell around his face always made me melt a little.

"You look gorgeous," he said, and the look in his eyes—they were definitely more green than blue tonight—was wolfish, as if he was appraising whether I might make a tasty meal.

"Um, thank you," I answered, doing my best to stand on legs that felt as if they might liquefy like Popsicles in the summertime. "You don't look so bad yourself. *Stranger*," I added, remembering that I had a bone to pick with Michael, that I was disappointed in him, *angry* even.

"Stranger?"

"You haven't been by in a while," I said.

"So you noticed?" he asked, smiling.

"Maybe. Too busy pleasing Veronica?" I asked, trying to sound like it wouldn't matter to me if he and Veronica might even be considering marriage. "Last time we saw each other you and Veronica shut yourselves in my bedroom for a heart-to-heart."

"Antonia," he said, a concerned look on his face, "I know you might have overheard some things . . ."

"I don't know what you're talking about," I said quickly.

"So you and Maria weren't listening in on us with your ears pressed up against the door?"

"Maria and I just happened to be standing there having a conversation. It *is* my room, after all. And we may have heard a few things, but if we did it wasn't intentional," I lied. "It's nice to see you finally," I said, changing the subject, and because it was true. I meant it.

"Is it?"

"*Yes*," I said, and smiled for the first time since he'd walked up to me. "I may have missed you a little," I admitted, becoming shy.

"Well, that's interesting news," he said, taking a step forward so we were closer again. For once, *for now*, I was enjoying being the object of his admiration.

"I was a bit . . . lonely. Before you got here tonight, I mean," I said.

"What? No Bishop Francis boys vying for your attention? That's a shock."

"Maybe a few."

"Only a few?"

"Well, just one."

"All the other guys are too intimidated," Michael said.

"Oh, whatever." Now, *that* was a ridiculous statement.

"I just speak the truth, Antonia," Michael said. "You have no idea, do you? The kind of effect you have on guys? You are, like, untouchable—you know, impossible to get."

"That can't be true since the guys at your school barely even give me the time of day."

"That's because the word at Bishop Francis on the matter of Antonia Lucia Labella is *Don't even go there*."

"I'm just waiting for the right person to come along and sweep me off my feet," I said.

"And who might that be?" He took another step toward me. "Is this going to be the night that I am finally going to get my kiss? Then I can top off my collection of HA girls," he teased. "You've made me feel so accomplished about it already."

"We're just friends, remember," I said, feeling bold, closing the last bit of distance between us, aware of how much I was enjoying that of all people it was me with whom Michael was talking and flirting, that this was what he'd been doing for years now, or at least trying to when I wasn't busy pushing him away. The thought of him with another girl made me feel jealous. The thought of him with *Veronica* made me feel insane. Had they ever kissed? Did they have some sort of . . . understanding . . . like Maria and John seemed to have, that when they saw each other they'd hook up but they just wouldn't call themselves boyfriend-girlfriend? I had to know. "So does your *collection* of HA girls that you've kissed include Veronica?" Please say no, I willed.

"Antonia," he said, his voice serious, "I told you: there is nothing between Veronica and me."

"You're avoiding the question," I pressed him.

"Okay. Once and for all, I have never kissed Veronica, there has never been anything between me and your cousin, and there never will be."

I wanted to believe him.

"Aren't those almost the exact words you used to tell Veronica the same thing about me?"

"I *was* right. You were listening."

"I may have overheard some things."

"I'm sorry, Antonia. I didn't mean what I said to her, but she wouldn't leave me alone and I wanted her off my back and I was afraid that if she knew she might do something in anger . . ."

"If she knew what?"

"I was afraid if she knew that there *is* this one girl . . ."
—Michael began, so close that I could feel his breath
warm against my neck, so close that I had no choice but to
drop all thoughts about Veronica to bask in Michael's
nearness and what he was about to say . . . realizing that
for once I hoped that it had to do with me—"that I've wondered about."

"Wondered what?"

"Wondered whether there's some chance she might
have feelings for me," he said, taking my hand. "In fact, I
haven't been able to stop thinking about her."

"Really," I said, as he took my other hand, and I kept
reminding myself to breathe as the music turned from fast
to slow.

"Do you want to dance, Antonia?" he whispered, sending chills down my spine.

"Sure. Yes. That would be great." My heart raced as he
led me by the hand, weaving through a path of couples already pressed against each other to a spot not far from the
edge of the crowd.

"How about here?" Michael said, turning toward me,
expertly guiding my hand up around his neck, taking the
other in his, pulling me close. His skin felt smooth and it
was hard to resist playing with the waves of hair that
danced against my fingers.

"So I was talking about this girl," Michael whispered,
but didn't finish. Little by little, his arms tightened around
me until we were dancing as close as the couples I'd

watched earlier that night, almost to the point where there was no space between us. We swayed to the music and I felt myself melting into the warmth of his body. I thought about how the Antonia who fought off all boys including Michael seemed to have disappeared, replaced by another Antonia, who wished that this slow song would never end.

But it did. Eventually.

As we pulled apart I was too nervous to look at Michael, so instead I glanced around, staring at anything but him, avoiding all thoughts about the fact that my body had virtually been welded to his for the last six minutes, which, *ohmigosh*, was so intimate and new and wonderful.

At which point exactly two unfortunate things captured my attention, shattering my bliss.

The first was Veronica. As soon as our eyes met I knew that she'd watched our entire dance, that she was fuming and had just confirmed that it really was me standing between her and Michael. She had that expression I knew so well—the kind she always got when my mother asked her to do something at the market that she didn't like or when Aunt Silvia admonished her about how eating that tenth cookie was not a good idea—that look where her lips were pursed and her nose scrunched up, creating little creases between her eyes.

It was Veronica's I-hate-you face.

A seed of worry planted itself in the pit of my stomach, but I refused to let it grow. I wasn't going to let her ruin my night.

Which was when I noticed unfortunate thing number two. Veronica was not the only person watching me — watching us. It was dark, but I could still make out the tall figure of a boy standing not too far away, an ugly smirk on his face, directed at me.

Andy.

"Um, let's move to the other side of the gym or anywhere but here," I said, feeling embarrassed, the spell of just moments before totally broken. I wished I could cover my eyes, as if that would prevent someone from seeing or finding me.

"Forget about him, Antonia," Michael said, his voice protective, when he noticed Andy's stare. "You deserve better. It makes me crazy to even think about how . . ." He didn't finish but he'd said enough. *He knew.* Michael knew what had happened between Andy and me. I wondered what version of the story Andy had spread around. What he claimed *really* happened. "Come on," Michael said, grabbing my hand to lead me somewhere, anywhere but where Andy could see me.

"He's just a jerk. I know that now," I stammered, not wanting Michael to think I still had feelings for Andy, *really* not wanting Michael to think I was interested in anything or anyone other than him at this moment. Because I wasn't.

When we reached the opposite corner of the gym I finally dared to take in the guy standing before me, the boy who was at once my friend and the person who made my heart thump like mad. His eyes, glimmering in the darkness, were intense and sweet, but most of all I knew they were only and totally, exclusively for me.

"Are you okay?"

"Never better," I said, willing myself to keep my gaze steady on Michael, not allowing myself to chicken out and turn away. For the first time in my almost-sixteen-year life, I had that *just knowing* feeling about how I wanted this night to go, kind of like that *just knowing* feeling I'd get when the pasta dough was ready, and that *just knowing* feeling that someday I really would become a saint. It was, like, a sense of destiny. Rightness.

Then I did something I never dreamed I'd ever do.

"So, Michael," I said, a smile spreading across my face even though my hands were trembling, maybe my entire body even.

"Yes, Antonia?" Michael's voice was hopeful. I liked that he called me by my name and not "love" in this moment.

"There's this place in my school . . ."

"A place? What place?"

"It's in the library actually."

"The library?"

"Yeah, the library. Have you ever been to our library before?" I knew it was a stupid question as soon as I'd said it. I was pretty sure that Michael had explored the dark corners of the HA stacks many times before.

"Well, sort of . . ." he said, a little embarrassed, neither of us needing any further explanation.

I wasn't about to let this put me off. We all had pasts, right? Mine was just rather unblemished. "Well, I bet you've never been to this particular place in the HA library, which happens to be my favorite place."

"Are you offering to give me a tour?"

"I am."

"Lead the way." He was intrigued.

We headed toward the exit, wading through the bodies of our classmates, some of them still pressed tight together, swaying, their feet rooted firmly in place, the upbeat music secondary to their desire to wrap themselves around each other. Others danced wildly in groups, here and there in pairs, mostly girls, and we did our best to stay out of their way even as we were about to get whacked in the head by Hilary's flailing left arm, or shoved as Lila jumped up and down haphazardly, calling out, "Hey, Antonia," as we passed.

Everything felt surreal, as if I were dreaming, watching myself from afar. Michael and I pushed through the double doors that led into the lobby, where crowds of students stood around in the bright fluorescent lights drinking soda and water, taking a break from the heat and sweat and dark of the gym, and made our way to the doors that led outside.

I can do this, I told myself, taking a deep breath as the doors shut behind us and suddenly everything went quiet.

It was just the two of us now. Michael and me.

25

We climbed the old, familiar metal staircase that wound high into the library stacks, the only sound coming from the swish of my dress as it brushed against the railing.

"I've never been up this far," Michael said, breaking the silence. I could feel him close behind me, his fingers near mine but not touching them. Our hands slid up the banister.

"Well, I'm glad I can at least show you something new," I said, only half joking.

"You are full of surprises sometimes, Antonia." Michael's footsteps were heavy on the steps as we neared the top. "That's one of the things I love about you."

"No," I corrected him, "I'm as average as you can get." Except for the saintly aspirations, I thought but didn't say out loud.

"If you are anything it is definitely *not* average." His

voice was soft, sincere. I was still unaccustomed to sincere Michael—only flirty, funny-guy Michael.

Except for the bare bulb glowing above the landing, the entire floor was dark. I had never been up here this late. The stained-glass windows against the back wall that were colorful and bright during the day were as black as the night outside.

"I guess they don't expect anyone to do research during the Winter Formal," I said with a laugh, trying to conceal how nervous I felt, stalling near the dim light above the staircase as if I were afraid to move farther into the shadowy stacks, as if I didn't already know this place so well that I could get us where we were going blindfolded.

"I *doubt* it," Michael answered. His voice trailed off, both of us leaving unsaid what we knew about the real use for the library after dark by our classmates.

"Maybe we shouldn't be up here, then." Maybe we should turn back now, I thought. My earlier resolve was wavering now that we were here. Alone. In the dark.

"You can go back, but I plan on looking around," Michael said, taking a step forward, peering around the corner of one of the tall stacks packed all the way to the ceiling with old, musty books. "I've been offered a rare window into the secret life of Antonia Lucia Labella and I'm not leaving until I've seen through it."

Come on, Antonia, I cheered myself on silently. This would normally be the moment I'd start praying to some saint, *any* saint I could think of, but not tonight.

"Come on," I said finally, heading left toward the aisle, my aisle, the one dedicated on both sides to everything I'd ever wanted to know about sainthood. I motioned for Michael to follow me. "I never really said anything about telling you secrets, by the way. You're making that part up."

"I'm still hopeful," he said.

We crept past row after row, the floorboards creaking with every step. I thought about how just minutes ago we were pressed together, dancing, his arms around me holding me tight. Since the music stopped we'd barely touched, not even by accident, as if our bodies were suddenly repelled, like two magnets flipped so they pushed apart. As if we were suddenly afraid to touch each other at all.

By the time we reached the farthest aisle my eyes had adjusted to the darkness. I could see the familiar outlines of the books I'd read and loved and read again. When I dared a glance back at Michael, I could make out every feature on his face, the gleam in his eyes, the curve of his lips, and I could see enough to know there was wonder in his expression, anticipation maybe, curiosity even, about how we had suddenly gotten here to this moment. That *I* was the one who had led us to this place.

"Come over here," I said, walking halfway down the aisle and turning to face him. He waited at the end of the row, watching me. I gathered my skirt and sat as delicately as I could manage to on the floor, crossing my legs underneath the petticoat, fixing the delicate silk taffeta around me.

"So tell me, then . . . what's so special about *this* place? Why did you bring me here?" Michael sat down across from me, his knees pressing into the folds of my dress. He began scanning the spines of the books packed together on the bottom shelf, running his fingers along the bindings.

"Well," I began, distracted by his nearness, "what's special about this place is what's *here*. You know, all of these books. Not just any books, I mean, but these in particular."

Michael perused the titles, glancing up at the shelves reaching all the way to the ceiling, most of them too far away to read in the dim light. "We are in the saint section, I take it?"

"Yes," I said, pulling one of the thicker green volumes from the shelf, titled *A Biography of the Saints*. I opened it in my lap and tried my best to explain. "See, all of these on this bottom shelf are biographies of the saints, like this one—well, *hagiographies* really—since they are a bit embellished."

"Hagiographies?"

"Most saints have a hagiography of some sort. It's a story about their life that makes them seem kind of like, well, a superhero, but, you know, a *religious* one. It tells of all their miraculous deeds. That kind of thing."

Michael leaned forward to get a closer look. His knees pressed into mine and I felt a shiver throughout my body, beginning in my middle and flashing outward to the tips of my fingers and toes and running up my spine.

"You've read all of these?" He looked at me with his eyes raised.

"I have."

"Why?"

"Well . . ." I paused, thinking, deciding it was now or never, that maybe it was okay to tell Michael my odd-ball aspiration so far known only to Maria and Gram, and, well, maybe the Vatican. "You said you wanted a window into the secret life of Antonia Lucia Labella. Well, this is it." I ran my fingers along the spines of the books to my right, looking at the titles, then turned back to face Michael. "The key to me is all around us. Right here."

"What is it about the saints, Antonia? Why do they fascinate you so much?" His voice was soft, almost a whisper. He leaned closer. "The statue in your room. That binder filled with pages and pages, each dedicated to a saint, and those other binders up on that shelf, seven of them, I think. I counted that day I was in your bedroom."

"The thing is," I said, taking a deep breath, closing my eyes. "The thing is, I want to be one someday." The words escaped my mouth like the relief of a long-held breath under the ocean waves, a confession I'd been waiting so long to make but just needed to find the right person to hear it.

"You want to *be* one?"

"Yes. I know that must sound crazy, but I've just always wanted to be a saint. The first living saint in Catholic history, to be specific." I said this as if I'd practiced it, as if I went around all the time telling everyone my religious career goals.

"The first living saint?"

"Well, I definitely don't want to be a dead one."

"I don't want that either," he said, laughing. "Who else knows?"

"Just Gram and Maria. And now you," I said. "So those books you're so curious about—the ones in my room—you know, with the saint pictures in them? Those are my Saint Diaries: the chronicles of all my dealings with the saints, petitions, letters to the Vatican, stuff like that . . ." My voice trailed off, worried he might think I was totally mad.

But Michael took what I'd just handed him—the words expressing my deepest, most secret desire—without sarcasm or disbelief. He didn't laugh or say it was weird or break the enchantment in the air all around us, encircling us, so that everything—the dance, our friends, school, life, the market—simply disappeared and there was only him and me. He took it all in, this thing that was so much of who I am, and let it sit there between us, like something delicate that with a single breath might disappear or fly away, and *I knew*, I knew in that moment, what I'd been waiting for all this time.

"Why do you want to be a saint, Antonia?"

"That's a long story. Almost eight years long, if you want to count."

"I'm listening. How about the short version? Please? We can save the long one for later . . ."

"The short version . . . well . . . it's just that I experience the world as a miraculous place. I see *them*, I see them everywhere. You know. *Miracles*."

"And?"

"And I want to be a bringer of miracles."

"What kinds of miracles?"

"Oh, if you only knew," I said, laughing, wondering what Michael would say if he knew I'd lately proposed a Patron Saint of the First Kiss and Kissing.

"Tell me."

"I've already confessed enough for one evening."

"Well, maybe you already do."

"I already do what?"

"Bring miracles into the world."

"That's a sweet thing to say . . . but . . . *no*," I said, pausing, thinking about what he'd just said. "Though, if I do become a saint, someday I will have to have some miracles on my résumé, of course. Two, to be exact."

"Like I said, maybe you already do, Antonia."

"Maybe."

"Maybe," he said, his voice low.

"Ask me the question again, Michael," I said, hoping for courage, leaning toward him ever so slightly.

"What question?" His eyes were bright pools lighting up the dark.

"*The* question," I said, giving him a meaningful look.

"*The* question?"

"Yes."

"*That* one?" His voice filled with disbelief.

"Yes, *that* one. You know the one I'm talking about."

"I do," he half stated, half posed as a question.

"Ask me."

"Are you sure?"

"I'm sure."

"So, Antonia Lucia Labella, aspiring saint, girl whose window I haunt." He stopped. I could feel his breath just barely against my skin.

"Yes?"

"When am I going to get my kiss?"

"Now," I whispered as he raised one hand, brushing his palm along the side of my face, his other intertwining in the curls at the nape of my neck, guiding me forward until our lips were just barely touching. We stayed like that for just a moment, feeling each other's breath, the anticipation of a kiss held between us in all its mystery and thrill, when Michael finally, slowly, pressed his lips onto mine. How surprised I was to feel that they were soft and the hand making its way deeper into my curls pulled me closer and his lips were gently pushing mine open, open, open, until our mouths were both wide, until I knew for the first time in my life what it was like to be kissed, *really kissed*, movie-star-kissed, the tickling, sensuous feeling of his tongue on my lips, in my mouth, then our tongues intertwined, and suddenly I was sighing out loud because it all felt so wonderful and I just. Couldn't. Help it.

I was KISSING Michael McGinnis and there was nothing else in the world that I wanted more in this moment than Michael's mouth on mine and mine on his and our tongues and OHMIGOSH I was finally getting my first kiss and it was PERFECT because it was with the PERFECT BOY and for the first time now I reached forward to put my arm around his neck, pulling him closer because all I wanted was CLOSER when a spark like static crackled between us, making me feel faint, startled. And suddenly I heard footsteps clanging up the metal staircase and we quickly pulled back from each other.

What just happened? I wondered. Did *all* kisses feel like that? Like lightning?

"Antonia? Antonia!" A voice pierced the silence. It was Maria. I could hear her panting hard just a few aisles away.

"Um, Maria?" I called out, grabbing my skirt and starting to get up, still out of sorts about being interrupted.

"Yes, it's Maria. Antonia, ohmigosh, I'm so glad I found you." Her words came out in a rush.

Michael got up. Our moment was over. I'd made a mess of his hair, and I immediately reached out to fix it when really what I needed was to keep touching him, I never wanted to stop touching him again.

"Are you alone or with someone?" Maria called, still at the stairwell.

Michael grabbed my hand and pulled me toward the end of the aisle until we were both in full view. The smile on my face must have looked dreamy and dazed.

"*Oooohh!* Michael! Hello. I see you two have been . . ." Maria was staring from Michael to me when I realized there was lipstick—the red lipstick that I'd put on so carefully just a few hours ago—smeared all around Michael's mouth, and, I imagined, mine as well. Michael and I stood there holding hands, presenting ourselves as a couple to my best friend for the first time, as if we were waiting for congratulations. I must have had FIRST KISS written all over my face.

I wondered if Michael could tell. If he'd known.

Maria raced toward us, still breathing hard, shuffling through her purse and pulling a tissue from somewhere deep inside, pressing it into my hand. "Wipe your face, Antonia, and make sure you get that spot by your ear."

"What is it, Maria? What's wrong?" Panic rose inside me, replacing the euphoria I'd felt just seconds ago from kissing Michael. "Did something happen with John?"

"Don't freak out, Antonia," Maria said, pronouncing each syllable carefully, as though if she went any faster I wouldn't be able to understand, "but your mother's downstairs in the gym looking all over for you. It was Veronica. She went to your house or something. I don't know exactly what happened but I had a feeling you might be up here . . ."

"My MOTHER?" I shouted, dropping Michael's hand as if it were on fire, dragging the tissue across my face, trying to remove any trace of lipstick, of KISSING, that might remain. As if it would somehow help. "Veronica?"

"Yes, your mother, and yes, Veronica," Maria confirmed, grabbing my hand, yanking me toward the stairs and away from Michael. He stayed behind, his expression confused, disappointed, watching me as I and my beautiful red dress disappeared back down the rickety stairs onward to what was surely my doom, and away from the moment, that perfect moment, when my lips and his finally, *finally* met in a single, long, delicious kiss.

26

My Mother and I Personally Experience All of the Top Five Ways Italians Express Love in One Sitting

I *hated* Veronica.

I paced in front of the old wood stove in our living room, too upset to sit, still in my dress. I was waiting for my mother to come out of her bedroom, where she was "thinking" about my fate. The wait was excruciating. All the lights were on, the lamps on the side tables and the old chandelier overhead, as if my mother wanted to ensure that when she was ready to talk, she wouldn't miss even a single, telling flinch of my body, or suspicious flicker of my eye.

I was so grounded. So. Grounded.

There should be a Patron Saint Against Getting Grounded, I thought, tuning out the yelling and cursing in Italian coming from my mother's bedroom. I consoled myself that if the Vatican didn't go for the kissing specialty, maybe this could be my next proposal. They loved saints who were against things—against demonic possession (perhaps a saint I should start praying to on behalf of my mother), against wild beasts (mental note for future reference: I wondered if boys like Andy count as wild beasts?), against scurf (no idea what scurf is—perhaps some sort of disease?), against scrupulosity (whatever *that* is—against having scruples? Aren't scruples supposed to be good?) And then one of my all-time favorites, the Patron Saint Against Twitching. Should you find yourself with a little twitching problem, St. Cornelius is your man.

Alas, there was currently no Patron Saint Against Getting Grounded, since if there was I would have been praying to him or her fervently from the very moment that Maria led me back down the stairs and out of the library. In between feelings of fear I kept thinking: My first kiss! Finally! For the first time in my entire fifteen years and counting career as a girl, I'd been kissed! And well kissed. Movie-star-kissed. By a boy who *really, really* liked me. And how? *How* did I not realize sooner that Michael was *The Boy*? And when? When? I wondered, would we get to kiss again? My mother was waiting to tell me that I wasn't leaving the house again for social reasons until I turned eighteen.

Would I really have to wait for my second kiss for more than two years?

I was hoping Ma would cut the sentence back to seventeen.

Have I mentioned yet how much I hated Veronica?

Not only had she told on me, but she was waiting with my mother to witness the scene when Maria and I arrived in the lobby. I wanted to scream when I saw her, arms crossed, a smug look on her big Italian-nosed face.

"There they are, Aunt Amalia," she exclaimed, pointing at us. "Thank the Lord," she added dramatically.

"Veronica really has it in for you, Antonia," Maria muttered as we crossed the lobby.

"That's the truth," I whispered back, holding my head up, determined not to cry or look frightened, depriving Veronica of any additional satisfaction to her already obvious and odious triumph at breaking up my tryst with Michael.

"We were so worried, Antonia," Veronica lied, faking concern. My mother looked ready to explode. "I'd just driven over to your house to suggest that your mom and I could bring some spinach pies and cookies over to the Romanos for your girls' night with Maria. You know—*as a surprise*. And she thought it was a great idea so we hopped in my car and drove off. But then Mrs. Romano told us that you both were at the dance." She was unable to hide the wicked gleam in her eyes. "So we rushed right over to make sure you were okay. I'll let your mother fill you in on the rest," she added, turning to go.

"Thanks so much for the concern, Veronica," I spat, pretending to lean in to give her a hug goodbye and whispering in her ear, "There'll be payback for this, Veronica. I swear to you."

And there would. I meant it. Someday . . .

At this point my mother explained the many reasons why she was beside herself, which included the fact that

257

not only had I (a) snuck out via Maria's house which to her was unthinkable, (b) gone to an event I was forbidden to go to, and (c) put my idiot cousin in a position to embarrass my mother by knowing more about my whereabouts than she did, *but in addition to all of this* (d) when she arrived to humiliate me in front of everyone I know and don't from both HA and Bishop Francis, I was nowhere to be found, *and then, finally,* (e) in her hunt for me she came upon Maria, who basically had her tongue down John Cronin's throat and vice versa. So in addition to ruining my life and deciding that both Maria and I were fellow *puttanas*-in-training, she was making a stop on our way home to inform Mrs. Romano that Maria was all but having public sex on the dance floor.

I tried to talk her out of it. To no avail.

"All these years I've thought Maria was a nice friend for my little girl and then I find out she's having sex with a *boy*!" This was my mother fuming to Mrs. Romano when she dropped off Maria on her way home to scream at me.

"Mom! They were *just kissing*," I protested, giving Mrs. Romano a don't-listen-to-her-please look.

"That didn't look like kissing to me!"

"Not like you'd remember," I muttered under my breath.

"Antonia! What did you say? This is not the time to answer back to your mother!"

Luckily, Mrs. Romano was a little less uptight than psycho-lady.

"I apologize again, Amalia Lucia," she said, shaking her

head in what I hoped was false solidarity with my mother. "I didn't realize that Antonia wasn't allowed to go to the dance. And I'll be having a chat with Maria. Thank you for bringing them home," she added, closing the door, leaving my mother and me outside on the steps. "Maria! Come down here now!" Even through the door I could hear Mrs. Romano yelling.

"Good thing I was able to let Cara know her daughter is headed down a road of carnal sin!" My mother spat the word *sin* as if it were a pestilence as we walked back to the car.

I finally heard my mother's footsteps padding down the hall, and she finally emerged into the living room. She gave me a look of death as she settled in to give me a good dose of serious Italian mother-love.

"So, how long am I grounded, Ma? For real. *Please tell me*," I begged.

"I told you," she growled from the antique chair where she sat like a queen presiding over one of her rebellious subjects, i.e., *me*. "Until you go to college."

"Amalia Lucia?" Gram's voice called from the kitchen. "Might I have a word?"

"What do you need, Ma? Antonia and I are having an important conversation."

"That's what I wanted to talk to you about actually."

"Well, don't do it from the kitchen."

"Are you sure? I just thought . . ."

"Ma, just come in here. Say what you have to say."

"Okay," she said, shuffling in wearing her fuzzy blue

slippers and robe, her hair in curlers. "I thought you might want me to say this to you privately, but since you insist" — Gram paused to take a deep breath — "I wanted to remind you that when you and Gino started going out on dates you were fifteen, just like Antonia."

Insert my mother's reddened, angry face *here* and my eternal gratitude to Gram *here*. Score one for Gram. She may have not remembered what happened last week, but she sure remembered every detail from twenty-five years ago.

"And I know it's difficult to see her all grown up so quickly, what with Gino gone and you raising her all alone. And then she's turned out so beautiful, especially in that gown — you'll have to tell me where you got that later, Antonia — which must make you think about how maybe someday soon *she* will meet *her* Gino." Gram was on a roll. "And then your baby will be off before you know it and you'll wonder where all the time went and you'll miss her so much you won't even know what to do with yourself."

Was that a tear rolling down my mother's face? And one rolling down Gram's too?

"I know you must be so angry at her for lying to you tonight, which was *wrong*," she said, giving me a stern look, "but I think it's time, sweetheart, that you started to trust Antonia Lucia. She's a good girl. A smart young *woman*. I remember how hard it was for me to let you go out with Gino, but I knew you would make good decisions. And I know deep down you believe the same about Antonia Lucia."

I stood frozen now, my attention bouncing back and forth between Gram's speech and my mother's anger dissolving into teary affection, for who—me or Gram or both—I wasn't yet sure.

"I'm so sorry, Mom," I said once I was sure Gram was finished. "I just really wanted to go to the dance—I swear it was my first one—and I'll never go behind your back again—"

"I remember what it was like to be young, too, you know," my mother said with a deep sigh, her voice wistful. "And worrying that your grandmother wouldn't let me go out with your father because he was older and I was still so young."

"You do?" Now *I* was tearing up.

"And I know your grandmother is right, that I've been too strict with you."

"Really?"

"I'm going to have a spinach pie," my mother said, since they were on the coffee table still sitting in the bag with the cookies, and since when Italians are in distress we eat. "Do you girls want one, too? They're so fresh. Just out of the oven. I was making them while you were at the dance, Antonia," she added, giving me a wry smile.

"I'll be right back," Gram said, waddling off to the kitchen and returning with a stack of plates and napkins, at which point we tearily proceeded to devour the entirety of the bag's contents.

"Be careful not to drip oil on that dress," my mother said in between bites. "You *do* look lovely."

"You think?" I smiled wide and then hoped that I didn't have spinach stuck in my teeth.

"Next time you need to get dressed up, though, your grandmother and I will find you something *really* special," she said, with some haughtiness.

"So there will be a next time?" I asked. She ignored this question, however.

"You know your grandmother used to be an incredible seamstress. She used to make Italian lace. I'm sure she still could."

"I know I could," Gram said. "That's the kind of thing you never forget how to do. Like riding a bike." Of course, Gram had never ridden a bike, but still, she made her point.

"*Next* time"—my mother was getting excited now—"we'll have to make you a dress, won't we, Ma?"

"A beautiful one for my beautiful granddaughter," Gram agreed.

"We'd have to find a way to fix your lack of cleavage, though," she said. "The family bosoms seem to have skipped a generation."

"I could just sew in some inserts . . ."

"Could we please get off the bosoms subject?" I pleaded. "But I'd love it if you and Gram made me a dress, especially if you'd also let me wear it out somewhere, like the prom," I dropped hopefully, since I figured that at this point, what did I have to lose? Our conversation had taken the last turn I'd expected, thanks to Gram.

"Well, I'm going to bed," Gram said, yawning suddenly. Then she gave me a big smile and disappeared from the room as quickly as she'd entered. "Good night, my two sweethearts," she called back to us.

"Good night, Ma," my mother responded.

"I love you, Mom," I said finally, looking into my mother's tired eyes. It was late and time for us to go to sleep.

"I love you, too, Antonia Lucia, *bella mia*," she said. "But you're still grounded for lying to me and sneaking around." She mustered a stern tone in her voice again.

"Until college?"

"Maybe not college," she said, a little smile on her face. "O *Madonna*, I need this day to be over. The drama!"

"Me, too," I said, giving her a kiss on the cheek. "Good night, Ma." I watched as she headed off to her room, still teary-eyed. For the first time since I was little I thought there might be good things to come between my mother and me. And I couldn't wait to see what they were. Especially if they included hand-sewn dresses of beautiful Italian lace that I could wear somewhere with Michael!

Underneath all the fighting, the screaming, the guilt, the melodrama, and, of course, all of the endless eating, I thought, as a yawn escaped me, there really *was* love after all.

27

I Learn Surprising News About My Reputation and I Hope that the Second, Third, Fourth, and Maybe Even The Fifth Time Is the Charm

Michael and I sat across from each other on my bed. Between us lay my Saint Diary, open to the section where I kept my proposals to the Vatican. Petitions, some long, some only a single line on a strip of paper, were strewn across my quilt, mixed among photographs of me from when I was eight, twelve, and from just last month. A white candle sat on a metal tray with a book of matches next to it.

"The Patron Saint of the First Kiss and Kissing," he said, surprise in his voice. This particular letter more than all the others fascinated him. He held it in both hands as if it were fragile, as if it were me or even my heart laid bare. He read the words, *my words*, taking his time, while I waited for him to finish and say something. *Anything.*

Michael was his typical, disheveled self again, even though he still wore the same clothes from the dance. His jacket was draped over the vanity chair. His tie was loosened. His shirt had a gray smear of dust from climbing through my window and standing in the shadows of my bedroom, waiting, waiting, until I came in to sleep, scaring me to death when I walked into the room, shushing me so he wouldn't have to face the wrath of my mother if she found out tonight, of all nights, on top of everything else, that I now had a boy in my bedroom.

"I couldn't just let the night end there, Antonia," he'd said to me eventually.

I'd agreed.

The skirt of my dress spilled over one side of the bed in waves of taffeta, iridescent in the soft glow of the candlelight near St. Anthony. After finally confessing everything, the whole story of my aspirations for sainthood, and showing Michael my collection of Saint Diaries and all my years of proposals to the Vatican—I'd even shown him my formal ritual for petitioning saints—as he sorted through my saint paraphernalia he was supposed to think about who he wanted to pray to himself.

"Are you ready?" I asked when he put down the letter.

It was time for Michael to petition a saint, as he'd agreed to do. In my demonstration I'd thanked St. Anthony for helping me find my senses about Michael (he smiled when he heard what I'd said). I waited for him to flip to one of the pages in my Saint Diary—maybe St. Anne to ask for some further grandmotherly intervention to convince my mother that dating at fifteen was acceptable; or St. Barbara, the Patron Saint of Grave Diggers, so that he wouldn't be going to his grave anytime soon even though he risked life and limb by being in my room; or even St. John to express thanks that we were no longer "just friends."

But when Michael lit the candle between us and closed his eyes, my diary lay there, untouched. Had he chosen a saint that I didn't already know? One that wasn't in my diary? He sat there, eyes closed, unmoving, for what felt like an eternity. Why wasn't he making his petition out loud like I had? I'd spent all night confessing my deepest secrets and now he was going to hold back this one little prayer?

"You look angry, Antonia," Michael teased. "What did I do wrong between the time I closed my eyes and opened them again?"

"Well, first of all," I said in a whisper, "you didn't choose a saint representation to pray to like I showed you. And second, you decided to keep whatever you asked for to yourself and that's not fair. Petitions aren't birthday wishes, you know."

"But you're wrong," he said, grinning.

"No, I'm not. It doesn't matter if other people know what you pray for, whereas with birthday wishes . . ."

"That's not what I meant," he said.

"Okay. So, then . . . enlighten me, please."

"You're irresistible when you're angry."

"Now is not the time, Michael."

"All right, sorry. I'll stay on task," he said, laughing, taking my hand in his. "I *did* choose a saint representation *and* I had every intention of telling you about my petition

. . . it's just that I needed to do some explaining before you'd understand."

"I'm listening," I said, as he ran his fingers across my palm and the back of my hand.

"So there's this rumor going around the neighborhood."

"Oh, no," I said feeling dread.

"Let me finish. This is important." Michael put a finger to my lips, silencing me gently. "Rumor has it that Federal Hill has its very own saint-in-the-making. That a local girl—still only a teenager, according to some—has shown herself to have a miraculous effect on those she touches . . ." he said, pausing, my curiosity rising. "Or, rather, *kisses.*"

"What?" I was confused. "Who?"

"Don't you know, Antonia? Can't you feel it? The effect you have on everyone around you? I wasn't just giving you a line back in the library about how maybe you were already making miracles happen. I meant it. And according to neighborhood sources, your miracle count is somewhere around ten, with one major miracle among them: Mrs. Bevalaqua."

"You mean *me*? Me? Are you crazy?" Had my whole neighborhood—if Michael was telling the truth—gone *pazzo* (that's Italian for "crazy")? I thought back to the strange incidents over the last couple of months—from Mrs. B walking again to the little cuts and bruises of kids like Billy Bruno and Maria's little sister, Bennie, healing almost instantly. People thought I might be a saint? *Other people?* Could it be true? Was that why children had been following me around the neighborhood, whispering?

"Yes, you, Antonia Lucia Labella. It's almost un-canny—that letter about being the saint for kissing you wrote to the Vatican—as if you somehow knew . . . *and* if I did my homework right, between the miraculous events and your growing local fame, I think you're practically the Patron Saint of the First Kiss and Kissing already."

"But I was talking about a whole different type of kiss-ing in that letter."

"I don't think it has to be one or the other," he said, leaning so close now that I felt the world disappear, like it had earlier in the library, when we'd been about to kiss. I smiled with anticipation. "I *hope* it doesn't. Don't you agree?"

"Yes," I said. He could have convinced me of anything just then.

"Good."

"So if you really believe this . . . why don't you ask me the question again, Michael," I said, grinning.

"*That* question?" he asked.

"*That* one. Yes."

"But I already did," he said, our lips so close they al-most touched. "When I closed my eyes I made a special pe-tition to Antonia Lucia Labella, the Patron Saint of the First Kiss and Kissing, who is not only stunning in that red dress but is also sitting before me. I wondered if she wouldn't mind terribly, and if it was still within her area of specialty, that I might have the honor of a second kiss, and maybe a third and fourth and so on." His voice was a whisper. "So, St. Antonia . . . when am I going to get that *next* kiss?"

"Now," I sighed, just before our lips met for the second time that night, eager to find out whether second kisses, and thirds and fourths, were even more divine than first ones, thinking that I might not be an official saint *yet*, but feeling confident I was on the right path. Especially since I was sure it was going to require many hours of kissing practice before I'd *officially* be ready for the job.

I was going to *love* being a saint.

Vatican Committee on Sainthood
Vatican City
Rome, Italy

December 25

To Whom It May Concern (ideally the new Pope if he's available):

First of all, I hope you are enjoying your first days as our new Holy Father. We are all excited to see what changes you will bring.

And I also thought, on this special holiday, that it might be appropriate to tell you about a Christmas miracle, really the best miracle a fifteen-year-old girl who is also aspiring to be the first ever living saint in Catholic history—the Patron Saint of the First Kiss and Kissing, to be specific—could ever hope for. (That girl in question would be me, Antonia Lucia Labella, of Labella's Market in Federal Hill, home to the most famous homemade pasta in all of Rhode Island.)

I got my first kiss!

And let me just say that it was *truly divine*. (Imagine me sighing happily here. Don't worry, I'm still as innocent as I ever was. Well, *almost*.)

I don't know if this means anything significant

for my possible sainthood, but, truth be told, I'm not sure I need it to. (Feel free, if you are confused about what I'm talking about here, to check the more than eight years of documentation about my quest for sainthood—you should have it all in my file.) My family, my crazy wonderful neighbors, my new boyfriend (!!), they all sort of make me feel like a saint already.

It isn't exactly how I imagined sainthood. But it feels right. For all I know, we've all got a little saintliness somewhere deep inside our souls. The possibilities are endless. Why should I be any different, then?

So I've made an executive decision: No more proposals. No more e-mails. No more pestering. You have a lot on your shoulders right now, what with learning how to be the new Pope and Fathering the Fold and all. And if sainthood is truly in the cards for me, I'm content to wait and see what happens (even though patience has never been my strongest virtue).

And don't worry, this doesn't mean I'll stop petitioning the saints we already do have. That would *never* happen. After all, I've got a lifetime of faith in all those women and men who've gone to the great palace in the sky. I couldn't imagine the world without their miracles.

Anyway, that's all for now. Oh, and have a Merry Christmas!

Blessings,
Antonia Lucia Labella
Labella's Market of Federal Hill
33 Atwells Avenue
Providence, RI USA
saint2b@live.com

Acknowledgments

A special thanks to Beth Wright, the first person I told about Antonia's story and who never let me forget about it until it was done, and to Pooja Makhijani for reading and rereading drafts. My gratitude goes out to many others, especially Tanya Lee Stone, Emily Franklin, Stephen Prothero, Lauren Winner, Beth Adams, Chris Tebbetts, and everyone associated with the writers' retreat Kindling Words, at which I received the encouragement and energy to believe in my ability to write *this* novel. To Frances Foster, who I told everyone was my dream editor, who somehow then became my real-life editor—thank you for your incredible editorial guidance, support, sense of humor, faith in this story, and the "possibility of me" as a novelist, and for really being a dream of an editor. To Miriam Altshuler, my agent, who believed long ago and well before I did that I was really a novelist, who loved this story from the beginning, and whose support for me as a writer is unbounded. To everyone at FSG, in particular Janine O'Malley and Robbin Gourley, for making this a wonderful experience. And finally, I have to mention my mom, whose childhood stories and life with the saints inspired this story, and Josh Dodes and my dad for being there through it all.